# AGAMEMNON MUST DIE

A retelling of Aeschylus' Oresteia

By

Hock G. Tjoa

4

# CONTENTS

# A Note on Aeschylus' Oresteia

(Spoiler alert! Those who do not wish to know what "happens" in this book should skip all front matter.)

The Oresteia is the only Greek trilogy that has survived to the present. It is said to have won first prize in an Athenian festival in 458 B.C. On the basis of fragments quoted or titles recorded, scholars know that Aeschylus wrote about seventy plays of which only seven have survived.

The trilogy was based on a popular group of legends surrounding the royal family of Atreus, king of Mycenae and father of Agamemnon and Menelaos. The two brothers were married to sisters, Clytemnestra and Helen (of Troy). When Helen was seduced and abducted by Trojan prince Paris, Agamemnon led a fleet of "a thousand ships" against Troy (ca. 1250 B. C.).

The Trojan War lasted a legendary ten years. When Agamemnon returned, he was murdered or killed in a fair fight depending on one's point of view.

In the second play of the trilogy, Orestes returns to Mycenae seven years later to avenge his father. He is accompanied by his sister Elektra and cousin Pylades, and urged on by the god Apollo, one of the "younger gods" from Olympus. After he kills Aigisthos and Clytemnestra, the Erinyes ("Furies," old earth goddesses) set upon him. Apollo finds that even he cannot protect Orestes and sends him to seek Athena's protection.

This is how the third play in the trilogy begins. It ends in Athens where the questions of Orestes' guilt and of the Erinyes' right to punish him are debated and adjudicated by a court consisting of Athenian men with Athena given the deciding vote. Aeschylus original focusses on the debate between the old gods and the Olympians.

The significance of the Oresteia for the development of Greek drama and of Greek and Western religious and political thought continues to be a subject of much scholarship.

I first read the three plays in the translation by Richmond Lattimore (1942, 1959), which seemed to me, then and now, to breathe tones worshipful of Greek civilization as interpreted by those like C. M. Bowra (*The Greek Experience*, 1957) and Werner Jaeger (*Paideia*, 1939-44). Lattimore thought Aeschylus had "perfected lyric tragedy," such that it had "never since" been so "completely realized" (p. 28). Bowra commented on the "unfailing magnificence of poetry" in the Oresteia, and declared that "the state [serving] as impartial arbiter [for murder] was indeed a momentous reform" (pp. 112, 113). In Jaeger's estimation (following Montesquieu), "the young democracy of Aeschylus' time is the perfect illustration ... that ancient democracy in its true and original form was based on virtue" (p. 240).

To that generation of scholars, it was indubitably clear that the trilogy told of the triumph of rational new gods over bloody-minded old ones and of the rise of humane, democratic justice from the barbaric cycle of death and vengeance.

Two generations of classics professors and scholarship have passed; the moral and political landscape has changed. I have not "kept up" with this research but in *Agamemnon Must Die* have told the story, selecting from variations of the legends of the House of Pelops (father of Atreus and Thyestes) and elaborating on characters as I felt would make sense and "connect" with a twenty-first-century audience. I have accepted as "given," most of the events that make up the "action" in the Oresteia. But Aeschylus did not have the monopoly of fact or truth even in his own time. Euripides, a younger playwright, shows us this in his plays, for example, in *Iphigenia in Aulis*.

Something ought to be said about the use of verse. In this book, it represents the voice of the choruses, the vision or dream of a character, or the declamations of various divine entities. The Olympians speak in six meters and the Furies in four, and everybody else uses free verse; I made these distinctions purely arbitrarily. In any case, the meters are English ones, dependent on stress, as opposed to classical

Greek meters that were constructed from short and long vowels. Those meters are very precise and impossible to imitate in English. Modern Greek no longer has such vowel values.

The spelling of Greek names in English should, I believe, follow Greek preferences, although many names are well-known not in that form. I have compromised by leaving all well-known names Anglicized (or Romanized). "Aigisthos" is so spelled because he is conventionally a minor character transformed in this retelling. But I have kept Ulysses as opposed to Odysseus and Hercules versus Herakles.

Let it be stressed that this is NOT a translation of the Oresteia. Gilbert Murray said that not even Milton "could produce in English the same great music." I have related the story that Aeschylus told with changes. The character of Aigisthos in this story is different from that painted by Homer or Aeschylus. I have placed Menelaos' return from Troy to Sparta six years after the war, despite Homer's authority for a delay of eight years. There are too many other differences to list. I hope the story is clear in this retelling.

Now, gentle reader, imagine yourself in Greece at the time of the Trojan War. Happy travels!

# IPHIGENIA

For three weeks this ominous summer in Greece, the winds gusted. The ships moaned, the seas roiled, and the skies remained dark, baleful, and gloomy. It was this doom-laden murkiness that gave the men gathered from every corner of Greece the hearts of goats scampering from a mountain lion.

Six seers pronounced the weather a temporary interruption of the season. Khalkas, the seventh, warned with dark, furrowed brow that they had offended the gods and must now sacrifice nothing less than a virgin daughter of one of the rulers. King Agamemnon spent all night rushing from chieftain to chieftain in the vain hope of persuading someone to volunteer a daughter. Rebuffed, he turned to Menelaus and the two brothers agonized whether cancel the war effort. Finally, the commander-in-chief offered his lithesome firstborn daughter.

Iphigenia was bright-eyed, dark-haired, and merry as the whistling larks of the air. Her younger brother and sister worshipped her like a goddess who led them with light steps in their daily chores and play. Her servants adored her as the sun and moon that brought warmth and light to their daily tasks with her willing hands and unfailing smile. To her mother, Clytemnestra, she was as precious as life. But with supplies running as low as the morale of the men, Agamemnon ordered the palace guards to bring his daughter—bound, gagged, and veiled—before him. The firstborn of the king and queen faltered a step as they led her up to the platform, but recovered to walk without resisting the guards. There, on a platform before the hushed troops, she gasped as her father unveiled her and slashed her throat.

A wild shriek pierced the gloom when the queen saw that the sacrificial virgin was Iphigenia.

The mother's cry—such a sound of love, loss, and anguish as had never been heard—pierced the heart of every man there as the princess splashed her lifeblood over the altar to the sand. The cry became a bitter, guttural moan as Clytemnestra ran up the platform and threw herself beside the warm but lifeless body of her child.

She could have looked forward to seasons of play and young love, and the many delicious decisions and rueful revisions she would now never make or unmake.

The queen's anger shaped itself into a snarl and then to a full-throated howl. The maddened sound reached through her loins into the depths of the earth as if to commune with Persephone, kidnapped by Hades. Then it ascended to resound in her womb, resonating in the belly that bore her firstborn and in the chest to which she had clutched her baby to suckle her milk-heavy breasts.

From earth through mother, the wail rose to the skies without a quaver of mercy or weakness. The cry was without hope. It ached and pierced the hearts of all present. It overflowed with pain and fury.

The mother's caterwaul continued and rang through the helmets of the champions gathered. She howled in grief and longing for the life that was now gone. She raged against her husband's willful drive to lead the Greeks against the Trojans. As she stormed in anger and anguish, the king signaled the armies to embark and set sail. The queen continued until her towering fury spent itself into sobs of resentful futility and she was the only one left on the beach in Aulis.

After the ritual slaughter of her daughter, the storm clouds dispersed. The king and his troops had gathered there in the gloom; it was now a brilliant sunny summer day in Greece as the ships sailed away.

Would the queen forgive or forget this moment?

The spray from the waves refreshed her even as it smelled like the tears now drying on her cheeks. No one dared look at her as she slouched her grim way with the small sending party on the journey back to Mycenae. One elder of the city, Aristides, more sympathetic than the others, roused himself to face her.

"My lady."

"Yes, counselor."

"Mourn your daughter on the journey to Mycenae, for when we arrive, you must rule."

# 1: THE NIGHT WATCHMAN

Ten winters passed since those ships sailed.

The ramparts and walls of the king's city loomed craggy and tall. For two hundred summers the walls of Mycenae and their tower, their vast blocks of stone rumored to have been built by the descendants of men and gods, kept a proud guard over the Argolid plain. Argos was the most important market town in the region, surrounded by villages and markets. Unlike Argos, Mycenae, the royal city, had an unobstructed view for five hundred paces all around. No one could remember its throne taken by attackers from the outside.

The watchman started as the first rays of the sun awoke him. The night before, he had drunk a large skin of wine, a gift from his neighbor's vineyard. Despite the sunny rebuke of his unintended nap, he smiled as he sniffed the air; he filled his lungs with the familiar and refreshing scent of daphnes that enlivened the days of late winter and early spring.

He had made himself comfortable in a corner of the huge, old rocks on top of the tower, and he drew himself erect among them, as befitted an old captain of the guards. The king had asked him to stay as captain in the city when the fleet sailed for Troy. Three summers later, he pleaded with the queen to relieve him of these duties, offering to serve as the night watchman so he could spoil his new grandchildren by day. He remained for another seven winters.

"I must remember to pick a warm west-facing wall or tower to lean against," he grumbled as he stretched his stiff arms and legs. "It is a good thing the wife made me bring my heavy cloak; may the goddess Hera bless her."

When the army sailed away, everyone expected it would return after a summer's fighting season. The former captain of the guards missed the comradeship of his men and the sense of being on the move. But one thing he knew, the city folk were as tired of the wait as he.

Peering over the countryside, he sniffed at the early morning smells. The fires were lit for the day's cooking and the watchman could recognize the aroma of hot wheat, barley, sour milk, and salt.

He hoped his wife had baked barley buns with bits of rosemary and would serve them for breakfast. The thought of those buns, eaten with figs or olives or cheese, made his mouth water. Soon, he heard steps approaching his lonely perch in the watch tower and turned to see the familiar face of his sister's son, a herald in the palace guard.

"Hello, Watchman."

"A good day to you, Agathon. You're come to keep an old man company or do you have errands that bring you up these walls?"

"I'm eager for something to do. I keep hoping you saw something."

"You are good to pretend I could see anything you cannot—"

"No, Uncle, I meant from up in this tower."

"I understand. To think when the war began, King Agamemnon said I should not go because I was too old. I hadn't even reached my fiftieth spring. And he told you that you were too young. Now you are more than ready, and I am weary of my duties even as a watchman."

The herald had trained with the guards for five summers already. His uncle had persuaded his parents to let him join and promised to watch over his training. They shared a facial trait; both of them had eye-brows that slanted upwards towards the middle of their faces. So, even though the watchman's eyes were dark brown and the herald's a light hazel, everyone guessed they were related.

The herald asked, "Who knew the war would last for so long?"

"Nobody," asserted his uncle. "We never fought for more than a few weeks at a time. I remember one campaign that lasted two cycles of the moon after we had brought in the harvest. We marched then against rebels when Agamemnon became king. That was the longest campaign."

"You never fought longer than that?" asked the youth who had grown to manhood with the armies away for ten winters, nearly half of his life.

"Even if we had to take on a handful of cities, our campaign would have been over before the winter chill," replied his uncle, scanning the countryside again. "We would be back before the men got too randy… starting trouble with the local women. If that ever happened, there would have been grumpy wives to deal with when we got back! Heh, you are not in a place to imagine such things, but that will come soon."

As the watchman began his morning exercises with his favored weapon, the spear, he gazed at his nephew. *The family must discuss marriage for this handsome young man with his muscular body, dark hair and unblemished tan complexion.*

The nephew remarked, "These last ten winters must have been a real trial."

"I couldn't have done it," blurted the watchman like a child who had not learned to lie. "Not go ten summers without my wife, nor she without me." He hefted his weapon and twirled it, end over end, to feel the comfort of well-practiced maneuvers as he limbered up for the day. "I cannot imagine that the king had to convince me not to sail with him. What was I thinking? I had served him and his father, old King Atreus, thirty winters by that time. Now I hope he returns soon so I may spend my days sitting in the sun. I shall watch my sons bring in the harvest, and my grandchildren skipping after the goats."

"Rumor has it King Agamemnon has taken some women over the seasons," said the herald like a hound bringing a kill to its owner.

"No doubt about it," replied his uncle with a broad smile. "Agamemnon is a lusty man. After their wedding ceremony, he and Clytemnestra kept the palace up the complete night and half the following week with their noisy nuptials. The servants say that the two of them only called for wine and honey all those days. What they received, they poured over each other and then lapped and licked from each other's naked bodies."

The watchman broke into cackling laughter even as he searched the young man's face and coughed, "Heh, perhaps you already know this." His tone carried a question.

"So, what does the queen think?" The young man said to parry his uncle's personal inquiry.

"Ah."

"I mean, you say there is no doubt about our king and his women."

"I understand what you mean. How does the queen cope? Well, everyone knows she took a lover many summers ago."

"Yes, Uncle. Everyone knows about Aigisthos," declared the youth. "He is someone of the royal family and accustomed to walking in and out of the palace unannounced. I thought there might be more gossip about what the queen thinks of the king's women."

"No, but some people tell dark stories, not about Aigisthos but about his father and his uncle, the old king." The old man now put away his spear and drew his sword to complete his morning exercises. He was one of the few who could fight with a spear or a sword. With his spear, everyone said the former captain was—in his day—more than a match for any two swordsmen among the guards.

Heavy footfalls tramping up the steps to the top of the city wall interrupted the two. Four soldiers arrived for the morning watch. "Ah, the watchmen for the day. Just in time, men. You know our young herald. He can't wait for genuine news, he says. You and he should keep each other well entertained."

"Oh, I'll be leaving," said the herald. "I shall ride out to where the new recruits are exercising. There's sword play I want to keep up with."

"Hm, I have heard about that. Heralds do not carry swords, Nephew."

"Perhaps I will not stay a herald for long. I want to see some real fighting."

"All that slashing and thrusting! It is not worthy of your ambition. I miss the company of those with whom I fought side by side. There is something soul-stirring in having shared the exultation of a charge or the terrors of a retreat." He fell silent as if lost in a horrible memory from which he soon shook himself, "As for those who live for the fighting and the killing, I know of such men. But I am not one of them. Now I'm off for the comfort of my wonderful wife and some sleep. How is your father with the pottery business?"

"Well, thank you," replied his nephew. "The war means a constant need for pots to ship olives, grain, and wine to our men in Troy. But my father will be happy for an end to this. He prefers to work on smaller jars with more decorations on them."

"Yes, my father used to grumble about his artistic inclinations; he worried that your father would become too distracted for ordinary pot making. I am grateful that both your father and my brother went into my father's pottery barn. They distracted the old man from his anger over my leaving the family business. Greet my sister for me."

# 2: THE BEACONS

Early the next morning, as the stars of the night paled before the sun rose, the watchman saw a distant beacon flame up on the Isthmian hills above the faraway city of Corinth. He peered to make certain it was not a trick of the early sunlight playing on his aging eyes. Then footsteps rang, and the herald arrived, panting with excitement, "Do you see it?"

"Only just," replied his uncle.

"We have won!" exclaimed the young man.

The old man spat over his shoulder, looking around the ramparts as if to make sure no one would overhear him, and said, "Don't be hasty. Ten winters is a very long time. The return of our men does not signify victory."

Agathon frowned at his uncle, who continued, "Besides, it is an unpredictable sail from Troy to Mycenae, a full cycle of the moon when all the winds are blowing in the right direction and all the rowers are fresh. The winds and the waves may yet swamp some who vanquished the Trojans."

The watchman shook his head as if a web of bleak thoughts fluttered around it. "The coming of the ships will also confirm many widows and orphans."

"You were not always so gloomy, Uncle."

"I have this old-fashioned belief that making too much of human happiness invites the jealousy of the gods," the older man responded in the tone of a father reluctant to inflict pain on a child. "We do not need that."

The two watched the light of the beacon grow stronger, more certain.

"Whatever the gods have willed, I shall announce the beacon to the court when morning breaks," declared the herald.

"Yes, do. The beacons have waited many winters to fulfill their purpose."

"How do they work?"

"The beacons? We probably built the first one on Mt. Ida, overlooking Troy. The guards would see its flames from a hilltop on the island of Lemnos. That's where the god Hephaistos fell, people say, when thrown out of Olympus."

"Who threw him?"

"Some say Zeus, others insist it was Hera. I don't know which. The watchers on Mt. Athos would see that and light their beacon so other mountain watchtowers across the north can do the same until that one, now sending its message to us."

"What will the queen do?"

With a heavy heart and a catch in his voice, the watchman said, "The guards and people I listen to expect that she will welcome the king,"

The herald blurted his next question, "And Aigisthos?"

The watchman hesitated, shifting his weight from one foot to the other. He said, "I do not think the king's problem will be with Aigisthos. It is more likely to be with the queen."

"But you said—" demanded his nephew.

The watchman sighed and shook his head and replied, "I said there are grim stories told about Atreus, the old king, and Thyestes, who sired Aigisthos. Ah, they were a robust and well-built pair!"

"I learned only yesterday that they were brothers," exclaimed the herald as children report a kiss or a quarrel in a neighbor's household.

"You've been checking up on me!" the watchman said smiling as he raised his hand pretending to cuff his nephew.

"Not at all," said his nephew, smiling also as he made an exaggerated move to duck the blow. "You told me that there were stories of gruesome deeds between them, so I asked around. No one wanted to talk about them. Maybe they don't know."

"They know," affirmed the uncle, picking up his spear for his morning routine. "The whispers started a long time ago, when I was too young even to think about joining the guards. They continued for many seasons."

"Did the brothers fight over a woman or something?"

"You mean, like the Greeks going all the way to Troy for Helen? Alas, it was about a woman, but also much else, much worse. Atreus was furious to discover that his wife Aerope was having an affair with his brother Thyestes. She was insatiable, I understand. But he was furious to learn that the two were plotting to cheat him of the kingship of Mycenae."

The old man sighed and shuffled his feet again, taking a deep breath before continuing, "It was a long time ago, two summers before hair grew on my face. I remember hearing that Atreus kidnapped his brother's young sons and had them killed and cooked for a dinner."

Agathon gasped at this revelation of an abominable deed from a bygone generation. His uncle paused and shook his head, "After the banquet, he asked his brother if he had enjoyed the food and then showed him the hands of the children and told him he could keep them as souvenirs."

"That's... monstrous!" The herald spluttered his horror and disbelief.

The watchman nodded and said, "Atreus was my king. I joined the guards a few summers later and served him for over twenty summers before he died. He always treated me well, but I agree with you as did the people of Mycenae."

"How did he get away with it?"

"Nobody wants to get involved in the quarrels of the royal family. Domestic disputes—" the old man said with a shrug.

"But you said the people of Mycenae—" demanded the youth.

"Thought it was inhuman, yes," agreed the uncle. "But it was not anything a man wanted to fight the king over. Have you not noticed that men and gods avoid getting entangled with the affairs of neighbors, especially if there is suspicion that they might be under some curse? Hercules himself, our greatest hero, got no thanks from anyone for rescuing Prometheus by killing the eagle that tore at his liver every day."

"Prometheus—was he the one punished for stealing fire from the gods and giving it to men?"

"Yes. Zeus himself was in a fury with Hercules, even though he did not destroy his favorite son," explained the watchman as he set his spear against the wall. He shrugged his shoulders like a parent giving in to its child's persistence for a treat or a plaything. "Anyway, it was up to Thyestes to avenge his sons. If he had led an attack on Atreus, he might have found support among the people.

What Atreus did was inhuman. You remember stories about Tantalus?"

"Only that he suffers in hell for doing something terrible."

"Legends say he stands tied to a stake in a lake with water up to his chin. Whenever he tries to bend to drink the water, the lake recedes. Just touching his head hangs a bunch of grapes, but whenever he turns his head up to get a bite, the grapes spring away." The old man said, like a story teller eager to speak of old tales. "Do you know what crime he committed to deserve this torment?"

"I can't imagine."

"He cut up the body of someone he didn't like, cooked it, and invited the gods to a feast for which he served this dish. This incensed the gods. They and men saw a lot more of each other at that time than now, and Tantalus had the bright idea of testing them for a developed sense of morality or at least of taste."

The old man smiled at his own sly humor, adding, "He found out. The gods have passed this story on to us humans as a warning and a lesson. I understand that before the gods sent Tantalus down to his watery prison, they gave him the 'gift' of immortality."

"So, his torment will last forever, ai!" The watchman shrugged and nodded; the herald continued, "I still cannot believe it. If people see evil being done, don't they try to stop it? Besides, why did the gods punish Tantalus with eternal torment and let Atreus off?"

"Perhaps there are different kinds of torment, Agathon. I am only a soldier and I don't pretend to understand these things. The gods mete out punishment that may appear unequal to us, but they see both before and after our lives and into our thoughts and souls. Punishment might take a form that is not clear to us mortals. Do these questions interest you?"

"Is that what happened?"

"What do the whispers tell you?"

"Nobody will tell me anything!"

"Those who, like me, remember the whispers, may prefer that the memories fade away," said the uncle.

"But you brought up these stories. Tell me, or the curiosity will choke the life out of me!"

"No one dies of curiosity Agathon, but the tale is worth telling," said the older man, shaking his head. "Atreus and Thyestes ruled

Mycenae together while the king was away dealing with some unruly descendants of Hercules around Sparta. He died during the expedition. The brothers thought they should inherit the throne and sought to gain the blessings of the gods by promising the sacrifice of a perfect lamb from their herds. Atreus found in his herd a lamb with a golden fleece—"

"The one Jason went in search for?" interrupted the herald.

"No, you're getting your legends mixed up," scolded his uncle. "Jason's golden fleece was from a magical ram that could fly. Atreus' was a lamb with a beautiful coat. But he decided he could not bear to part with it, so he asked his wife, Aerope, to hide it. That tramp gave the lamb to her lover, Thyestes, and told Atreus it had gone astray."

"Harsh on the queen mother, wouldn't you say, even though she is now long dead," said the young man.

"As I understand it, Aerope's father would have given her in marriage to anyone who would take her," said the watchman, waving his hands palms out towards his nephew. "He had caught the young nymph sleeping her way through the slave quarters."

"Oh."

"Strong, lustful desires run in that family, I guess," continued the elder. "Anyway, Thyestes then persuaded his brother to agree that they would search for the lamb, and whoever found it could rule alone. Atreus agreed, and Thyestes soon 'found' the lamb."

"Didn't Atreus suspect anything?"

The watchman nodded and continued, "Enraged, he whipped Aerope until she confessed to what she had done. Atreus confronted his brother with this confession, and Thyestes offered to step down if the sun should move backward for an hour. No one knows what Atreus did, but many whispered that through some sorcerers he persuaded the gods Hermes and Zeus to make it so and thus regained the kingship. And then there was that dinner."

"How did the sun go backwards?" demanded the herald.

"The gods do not disclose their secrets to the likes of me, Agathon. In fact, I only know about these events because my elders spoke of them to each other and I eavesdropped."

"That's how you learn things, by eavesdropping? Ha!" declared the young man.

"Well, if you talk only to your friends, you learn only what they know, which is not more than you. If you want to know more, listen to those who might not want to talk to you or to whom you rarely listen—your elders, your officers, your superiors."

"Sounds devious," muttered Agathon.

"Call it whatever you wish," responded the watchman with a smile.

The watchman and the herald looked at each other in silence. The herald asked, "Is this how you learned all these stories?"

"My parents were always busy working, like all our friends. And there were no servants or idle ones in our neighborhood to entertain us children. I think I heard most of these stories from around campfires."

"I can't wait to go camping and fighting!" declared the young man.

"There is much labor in the barracks and exercise grounds, and if there is fighting, there is always pain and blood," said his uncle.

"But there are always campfires and stories to share around them?" demanded the herald. His uncle nodded.

"So, how did Atreus die?"

"Someone killed him while he paid homage at the ancestral shrine." The old man paused again to gather up his arms and cloak from the night watch, before continuing, "I was there when it happened, but I don't remember more."

"What?"

"I was the only guard with him. As captain of the palace guards, I often was. Atreus thought he with his sword and I with my spear could hold off any attack short of a war. I had soldiers on horseback out of sight but within earshot. We were attacked, and someone knocked me out first. Then the old king and his attacker fought for a while."

"Didn't the troops examine the grounds?"

This outburst from the young herald prompted a smile from his uncle, who said, "Those who examined the grounds said the tracks showed there was only one attacker. When I awoke, our soldiers were all over me, but it was clear someone had clubbed me." The watchman paused and then added, "If I am not mistaken, whoever did this was careful not to kill me."

"What do you mean?"

"The attacker placed the blow that knocked me out well. A little to either side and it would have smashed through my skull."

"Who do you think did this?" asked the young man.

"I don't know. He attacked me from behind."

"What did Agamemnon do?"

"Nothing," replied the watchman with a tight smile. "He did nothing… He was getting tired of waiting. You can understand. He said nothing in all the seasons I served him after that event and before they all left for Troy. Not once did he question me about the death of his father."

"So, you think Aigisthos will not challenge him for the throne?"

"Aigisthos loved Atreus like his own father, and he followed Agamemnon around like a younger brother. He worshiped Agamemnon."

"And the queen…?"

The old soldier looked his nephew in the eye, "Most of the people in the city believe that she has never forgiven him the sacrifice of their daughter Iphigenia."

"That was ten summers ago when the armies sailed. Isn't it a long time to hold a grudge?"

"It is not a mere grudge when someone kills your beloved first-born child," said the Watchman. "To kill one's own daughter is despicable to our people. It is unholy to the gods, whatever the circumstances."

As the two prepared to leave the walls, the old man added, "I remember once or twice, when my father punished your mother, my sister, for some misbehavior. Your grandmother glared the entire time, even though she knew as he whipped your mother that he had a hot cloud in his heart. Our society has taboos about such doings. But it seems to tolerate an unfair burden of violence to girls. I only have sons, but I envy how devoted their wives are to their parents."

"So, do you think Agamemnon and the queen will fight over this?" persisted the herald. "Won't this draw Aigisthos in?"

"I try not to think about these things," muttered the former captain of the guards, like a horse that has never been in water balks at a stream. "My world is far from theirs, and so is yours. Try to remember that! We shall celebrate Agamemnon's return. But I think it will shed more blood."

The sun was halfway up to its zenith. Uncle and nephew made their way down into the city. Then the herald bade his uncle good day and left to deliver his news about the beacon to the queen and her councilors.

# 3: THE QUEEN AND HER LOVER

The herald delivered the message about the beacon to the queen and her entourage in the throne room. The sight of all the elders gathered awed him as much as the room itself always intimidated the young man. They built it of the same rock as the city walls and tower and appeared as old. The walls reflected a grandeur born of longevity and fortitude.

The queen was tall enough to look most of the elders in the eyes when most preferred not to have to look at her. She was ready to rule even as the fleet sailed for Troy; they would have liked someone more hesitant. Around her wafted a light fragrance, her favorite summer flowers simmered in oil by an ancient apothecary. In a composed voice she said, "We should prepare the city to receive the king. I imagine he will arrive with the next new moon."

"We will be ready," intoned the counselors. They could not conceal their eagerness for the king's return and the restoration of normalcy. Everyone in the city knew the elders resented the queen even as they accepted Aigisthos' attempts to smooth over their ruffled sentiments. Counselors who ruled their households with no consideration for what their wives thought found dealing with the strong-minded queen a sore trial.

"Make sure the purple cloak is clean, soft, and brilliant," Clytemnestra ordered her ladies-in-waiting while the elders were still making their way out of the room. "All the women of the palace have labored over it, while our elders never let a day go by without complaining about how much it cost."

"Yes, my lady."

"I'll order the men to prepare the games for his entertainment," said the captain. The queen and her lover had chosen him to replace the king's man. Both men would have accepted Aigisthos, but the former captain was not comfortable with the queen and her straightforward exercise of command.

When the men left, the queen retreated from the throne room as her mother had taught her—with her head high and giving nothing away by the look of her face or pace of her strides. Once through the doors, she stormed into the privacy of the royal chambers.

"By the gods," exclaimed Aigisthos, who sat by a window. "Is the day of wrath upon us?" The queen screamed in rage and frustration.

"How can you keep calm about that man?" she demanded. Her tanned face with a nose that sloped straight down from her brow darkened with unforgiving fury. "Me? With great difficulty and with the gift of the gods who must have had a guilty conscience," replied her lover with a smile on his friendly, open face. He looked much like Agamemnon with dark hair, large bones, and well-developed muscles. The fullness of his lips and a nose broken in a youthful brawl marked the differences between the two cousins.

The queen giggled, "I doubt you could exercise that gift when brought to Atreus' hearth as a foundling."

"Ah, then it was Atreus' guilty conscience at work, I suppose. Nobody knew who I was when they found me, but I think the old king felt there had been enough killing to add that of a baby. Fifteen winters later, when the nursemaid from Thyestes' household came forward to identify me, the gift of the gods worked its magic."

"You think the gods made you adorable to all because they had a guilty conscience?"

Aigisthos grimaced, shrugged, and lifted his shoulders and hands with palms up. "They did nothing to stop Atreus from chopping up my brothers and serving them to their father, his brother."

"Such monstrous impiety," cried Clytemnestra. "I still can't imagine it, though whispers of the story reached Sparta, and the maids talked about it as I was growing up. But Atreus lived to rule for twenty summers more. Does anyone know how he died?"

Her question hung in the air as Aigisthos weighed his response. "I do," he said. "I killed him."

His lover looked at him with wide eyes at this disclosure. She said, "We have never discussed this, but because no one ever talked about it, I assumed nobody knew."

"No one else knows," said Aigisthos. "I have told no one until just now. The old king was alone except for the captain of the palace guard, now the night watchman, and I had to knock him unconscious first."

"And Agamemnon?"

"He may have suspected something, but he did not order an inquiry. If anyone had asked, I might have confessed it then."

"I would not be surprised if Agamemnon had asked you to do it! I remember he was tired of waiting." The queen snorted with contempt at the memory of her husband's impatience. "Iphigenia was walking and talking, and I was pregnant with Orestes. We were not enough for his ambitions."

"Well, he did not ask me to do anything," Aigisthos said. Then he added with a knowing smile, "but for two summers, autumns, winters, and springs before that deed, he made sure I exercised daily with his best swordsmen and received extra coaching from his brother Menelaos. He often drilled me himself."

"That viper!" Clytemnestra exclaimed, disgust mingled with awe in her voice. "Why did you do it?"

"It is a complicated story. Soon after the nursemaid's revelation that this foundling was the son of the king's brother, left to die in the forest, I met my father in the marketplace. He badgered me for three winters about avenging my brothers," explained Aigisthos, wringing his hands with a frown. "I had never met or known them, and I loved the old king. In fact, I could hardly get over the fact that he was not my father."

He shook his head at the memory of meeting Thyestes. He could not believe the latter's story about his brothers. Even though he had heard vague whispers about that deed, Atreus had treated him like the youngest son in the palace. Agamemnon and Menelaos always accepted him as their brother—teased, mocked, made to take part in stupid dares and tedious errands, but always with the awkward affection of boys.

"Then he told me about my mother, my sister."

"Atreus killed them too?"

"No. It was that they were the same—Pelopia, my sister, my mother."

Clytemnestra was aghast. What a family she had married into! The confusion on her face reflected jumbled thoughts—one branch of the family of Atreus produced a king, her husband, who sacrificed a daughter to fight a war. The other, the king's uncle, unspeakably raped and impregnated his own daughter. She had pitied her sister Helen the shame she had to endure for running off with Paris, but this far outweighed that universal disgrace. She walked to her lover but stopped short of embracing him, pacing instead to the window, then turning back to him.

Aigisthos interrupted her thoughts, saying, "I never met her, for she killed herself in shame soon after she abandoned me in the forest, not more than a moon after my birth. She was only fourteen summers old then, I understand, but she knew what dishonor meant. I, on hearing about it, felt like the first time someone punched me in the stomach."

He shuddered and fought back the bile that rose to the back of his throat before continuing to tell a tale he had kept a private memory for fifteen summers. "My father told me that an oracle had proclaimed to him that a son of his would avenge his older sons, my brothers, but his wife could not conceive again. So, he tricked and raped Pelopia."

The queen's lover reached for his wine goblet and swallowed two huge gulps before continuing, "I agreed to do the deed, hoping it would be the last in the chain of vile deeds and gory consequences that has cursed this family."

The queen cupped his face with both hands and kissed his forehead. He continued his story. "Anyway, everyone in the palace knew Atreus and his movements. I followed him and the captain of the guards for some weeks, and then one day when the old king visited his ancestral shrines, I attacked them. I was fond of the captain, for he had taught me much and had made my life easier in a dozen ways. So, I made sure I struck him hard enough to knock him senseless but where he would suffer no serious damage." The queen held him closer, not daring to breathe as he continued,

"As I made sure the captain was unconscious, I looked up to see Atreus approaching. He grinned as he saw me but his eyes became cold, hard, and grim, as he drew his sword and said,

*So, my jackal of a brother has sent you.*
*I have loved you as my father, I said.*
*Yet here you are, replied Atreus.*
*Did you think it would be me? I asked.*

*He scoffed and said, I have waited these last twenty summers for someone to come at me. This breastplate has been my constant companion, and I have not eaten alone for all that time. Whether as guest or host, at every meal I let others taste every dish before me. Every night, I sweat and tremble in fear of news my guards might bring.*

*What happens now? I asked again.*

*What do you think? Are you afraid to raise your sword against me? There is no choice about this; we must fight, and one of us must die. If it makes any difference, I forgive you, Atreus declared.*

*The coldest midwinter gripped my head in a vice and a black fog filled my head as the old king strode away three steps before whirling around in the swift motion I knew so well. He drew his sword, so it hissed against its sheath, and he advanced like the lion he always was in battle. I moved to one side, so he had to change the rhythm of his attack, and I called out the last words I ever spoke to him—*

*Well, I have sworn a great oath before my father, your brother, and I cannot forgive you.*

*He strode, showing little of his age, and swung his sword with a force that would have felled any of the olive trees in the grove with a single blow. I was able, barely, to meet his sword, stroke for stroke. If we had time enough, I could have kept that up until he tired. But I was certain that other guards would soon come by just to check on his safety. So, I risked an all-out thrust at his chest.*

*He threw out his arms and bellowed a huge laugh as his breastplate stopped my sword. They made it out of some metal fallen from the sky, they said. My whole sword arm was sore for a week as the tip of my sword met the immovable object of Atreus' armor. But I quickly gripped my sword with both hands and thrust it upward into his throat.*

The lovers stared at each other.

"Was Pelopia the reason you never chose a woman for yourself all this time?" asked Clytcmncstra in a small, shaky voice. This queen, so feared and resented by many of the counselors, trembled as a woman in need of reassurance of her lover's inner feelings. Aigisthos pulled her into his arms, kissed her and said,

"No. She was my sister, silly. And remember, I never met her. Even before Atreus died, I had decided on the one for me."

"When?" she asked, pushing him away as she snapped out of her uncertainty. Aigisthos hesitated, suppressing a smirk as he reached towards a bowl of figs and said,

"When the old king brought his sons to Sparta to choose a bride from Tyndareos' house—they brought me along for the ride."

"Don't tell me you fell for Helen then?"

"Silly woman," chided her lover in a soft voice. "I saw two beautiful and happy girls, sisters and yet as different as night from day, one blonde and soft, the other dark-haired and commanding. Helen was ravishing, a pretty face. You," he said with a kiss, "make kings proud." Clytemnestra stammered and grinned as a blush crept up her face like the pink dawn in the morning sky.

"Well then," she said, regaining her composure, "what took you so long?"

Aigisthos laughed at the queen's mock severity. "Where I slept in this palace is a long story. When I was a baby, Aerope often brought me into their bed. This the servants have assured me. As soon as I was old enough to follow Agamemnon and Menelaos around, I remember I insisted on sleeping in their chamber. When the old king, expecting his sons' marriages, renovated and expanded the palace, he offered me a room nearby. But I told him I preferred to take one with the palace guards."

He reached for another fig before turning to face the queen and continuing, "There I stayed through the winter and summer solstices after the fleet left for Troy. I thought it the honorable thing to do to allow for the possibility that the Trojans might come to their senses and surrender Helen or that the war would somehow end."

"You kept the love of your life waiting on a point of honor—I like that," said the queen as she laughed with her hands on her hips. Then her mood darkened and her voice grew cold as she asked, "Do all good things end? What should we do when the king returns?"

"You are making fun of me."

"No, I did not mean to. But we must think about Agamemnon."

"I am sure he learned all about us when we sent Orestes and Elektra to go live with their aunt in Phocis," Aigisthos said. "I have decided I am not giving you up." The sun descended behind the hills and twilight crept over the city. He prayed, *please don't tell me to leave.*

The torch-bearers arrived and brought light into their chamber. The queen shivered as an evening breeze intruded; she reached for a cloak.

"I will never go back to him," she declared. "I cannot forgive him for the sacrifice of Iphigenia, and my heart has never stopped burning to kill him."

"You cannot kill him for that; it was a matter of state."

Clytemnestra sprang up vexed and pounded on her lover's chest, exclaiming, "What is it with you men? You would kill an innocent young girl so the gods will change the weather—just so you can then sail to some place, where most of the people have never heard of us, and kill some more?"

Aigisthos weighed the queen's outburst, then said, "No, not so. At many stages, people made choices. Perhaps they made bad ones, but they were choices defined by our traditions, by what holds us together as a society. What Paris did in seducing and abducting Helen broke the laws of hospitality that Zeus himself established. But Menelaos could have lived in shame for having lost Helen, and eventually both he and his city would have overcome the memory of the dishonor. They made the choice, however, to go with full-throated war-lust after Paris and Helen."

The queen's lover stepped to the window and gazed at the horizon. "When bad weather held up the ships gathered, Agamemnon could have admitted defeat. The gods had sent the clouds and the squalls—at the instigation we are told of the goddess Artemis. Perhaps the king might have tried to go a year later. Or he could have chosen not to go at all. But he chose instead to sacrifice his daughter. It was a terrible thing to do according to our customs, but our laws give fathers wide latitude over the fate of unmarried daughters."

As an afterthought, he added, "the lives of unmarried daughters are full of sacrifice." He cocked his head from one side to the other as if to clear it of thought, then he looked at the queen. "Now, you can forgive him—"

"NEVER!"

The queen's declaration rang through the room.

"You did not hold her at her birth, my first born. Have you ever smelled babies as they suckled or their breath as they smiled up at you? I fell as deeply in love with her—as I loved Agamemnon, and as I love you. Then the monster cut her throat." As Clytemnestra wound herself up in anger and vexation, Aigisthos wrapped his arms around her and kissed her over and over again.

After a while, he whispered, "Then let me do it."

Clytemnestra caught her breath and searched Aigisthos' face, his eyes. They were steady and, as usual, gave nothing away. "How do you give a calm and reasoned answer to every issue? Does nothing rattle you?"

"Many things frighten me even though I do not show it," declared her lover as he stepped towards the window again, his paces slow as he weighed his thoughts. "Just because I speak with assurance on this issue does not mean I have no doubt or dread on the matter."

"How am I supposed to know?"

"Would it help if you did?" Aigisthos smiled.

"I have seen you worried. But when you are as self-assured as now, I think there is nothing to fear. All these seasons I thought I knew you—I sense now I need to adjust."

The queen's lover walked towards her saying, "You know me, Clytemnestra. I have never put on an act before you. I promise I will try to be more obvious, if that is your wish."

"No," murmured the queen. "I think I have always understood you are careful to protect my feelings. I do not believe you ever deceived me, and I love you as you are."

# 4: THE PLOT

Later that evening, the servants removed all the torches except one, and left the lovers in their chambers. Aigisthos resumed the conversation regarding Agamemnon. Like old married couples, he and the queen companionably picked up the threads of each other's thoughts.

"I have to settle with Agamemnon over his queen, anyway."

"There are customs, conventions, and laws against regicide," declared Clytemnestra with a hint of slyness, as her wit struggled with her anxiety. "Don't our stories usually tell of killing the king *before*... the seduction of the queen..."

"Other customs and conventions would be on my side. The elders will think me justified in killing him because of what Atreus did to my brothers," Aigisthos continued, refusing to respond to his lover's distractions. "Twenty summers ago, when I killed Atreus, the city held its breath for a month to see if the house of Thyestes would extract more vengeance. That vengeance will now come as another, much later installment."

"But she was my daughter!" Clytemnestra bawled and howled as if to fill a burning void in her heart, her tears streaming as if to drown the pain. Aigisthos tightened his arms around her until the sobbing subsided then he kissed her, just as he had long ago when they overcame the taboos and fear of gossip and first allowed themselves to be drawn to love each other.

"The king and I have you to thank that there is not a withered woman pickled in hate and vengeance waiting here to kill him," declared the queen. "He would realize what he faced and would kill me first. For that, I thank you, Aigisthos. Now he will see me and think I have overcome my grief, perhaps even forgotten it. If the gods will it, I will kill him."

"The gods, the city, our society, will not allow the man who kills a king to go unpunished," her lover said. "But they will abide the vengeance of a man whose brothers have been slain and served as banquet dishes to their father, even if that foul deed had been committed not by the king himself but by the king's father, for the king gained from it."

"I doubt Orestes will see it that way."

"Did he not care for Iphigenia? Or does he love Agamemnon more?"

"All boys love their fathers more than they love their sisters. Agamemnon was a good father and especially favored his son. Orestes loves you too, but I don't think he and Elektra were pleased to be shipped off to their aunt when you started coming..."

"He is a good lad."

"What?" demanded the queen, now jealous over her lover's solicitude for her son.

"He is a good lad. Intelligent and well-intentioned."

"But...?" demanded Clytemnestra.

"But he lacks something that both Agamemnon and you have. I don't understand how it passed him by."

"What does he lack?" asked the queen.

"I think it is the courage or strength of will to be king," mused Aigisthos. "One needs to be beyond love and above humanity to wield power, or so I sometimes think. Yet he will come. Even if he has no desire to be king, he will come. Our customs require that he avenge his father and claim his birthright. The gods will hound him if he doesn't come."

"He would not dare attack me. I am his mother. There are even more dire consequences for killing one's own mother. The gods will haunt him if he kills me!"

"Perhaps the gods will fight among themselves."

Aigisthos thought this over after he said it and as he walked to the door of their chamber. He called to a servant to bring some wine.

"No, I will do this—kill Agamemnon as vengeance for my brothers, on behalf of my father. Then we should abdicate."

"Are you serious? What about ruling Mycenae?"

"People overrate being a king or queen. Haven't you come to the same conclusion? We will send for Orestes and tell him he can come and be king whenever he feels ready. No rush, he can take five or ten summers. This may divert him from trying to kill me. When he sends word, or we learn of his approach, we will leave."

"Are you sure that you don't want to stay and become king? The people would follow you; you know that."

"Tempting, but no. What I already have is more than sufficient for me, and I do not agree with those who see only morose mediocrity in life outside the palace."

"I would not be the queen you see here."

"I have never thought of you as a queen in my possession."

"Ah, the gift of the gods at work." Her lover beamed and nodded. She continued as she embraced him, "You make me very happy, Aigisthos. There is a tingling all over me, from the top of my head down to my feet. It is as if you make my toes smile whenever I think of you."

Her lover laughed, then grew grave and said, "I remember all the incidents and events as I grew up in Atreus' household and fought in Agamemnon's army. But now I cannot imagine that I lived all those seasons without you, and when I think of our lives and love, I can only think—more, I want more."

Clytemnestra glowed with contentment and declared, "Agamemnon was strong and masterful. He made me feel proud and overwhelmed me. You are as strong a leader and lover as he. You wooed me and gave me laughter."

Then the queen went into his arms and clung to him for what seemed a fateful time before arousing herself, sighing, "Alas, we must decide what to do about Agamemnon. Whether you do it or I do it, it is not easy to kill a king. There are steps that must precede the act, and there are consequences that will flow from it. What do you think?"

A maid came to the door with a flask of wine and two goblets. She poured out the wine and left. Aigisthos said,

"I think waiting would only give him time to get his bearings and the people of the city will get used to having him back as king. Killing him the first night he is here is best."

"How?"

"I will not trick him or poison him."

"He is a vigorous man and ten seasons of war have made him even stronger."

"I have no illusions. He will be formidable, perhaps even a match for Achilles. But maybe the voyage home has cramped his muscles or dulled his wits. Even if it were by a little, that would be helpful. But I do not fear him."

"I know you've been training; is that what gives you confidence?"

"I have practiced every day since before I took on the old king twenty summers ago. In the last few seasons, sometimes I sparred against two or three at a time of the best swordsmen left in Mycenae."

The queen sipped her wine as she weighed the outcomes from a battle between Aigisthos and Agamemnon. She said with worry in her voice, "I know you've also gone without food and sleep for days at a time. The captain of the guard tells me he and the sword-master worry about your practices during those times."

"I started doing that," Aigisthos said, "to honor the soldiers who've been away for all these seasons. I can't believe that such an immense army led by Agamemnon—with champions like Achilles, Aias, Diomedes, Ulysses—all together unable to overcome the Trojans for ten summers. There were so many of them, it made me wonder about the horrors the soldiers were going through."

He raised his goblet and emptied it with a gulp. "Those who died were lucky. The wounded have to deal with pains and fevers without a neighbor's touch or a kiss from the family. I don't understand how anyone remains sane in such a world—without pity and without hope."

Agitated, the queen's lover paced to and from the window, saying, "As for the supplies the army asked for, we have tried our best to send everything, but we did not always meet the quantities they required. When we could send the full requisition, we were never sure that the boats arrived whole or in time."

He stopped pacing and looked at the queen. "To skip a few days of food and sleep is a small token of respect for their courage to continue... to survive."

"The women who wait on me with husbands fighting in Troy have often been unable to conceal their anguish," agreed the queen, nodding.

"Then I learned that hunger and lack of sleep is a necessary part of a soldier's training, as it is an inevitable aspect of his life. So, decided that it would be part of my preparations for my meeting with Agamemnon. It is inevitable."

"When will you fight him?" asked the queen.

"As soon as they leave us alone."

"He will be on his guard."

Aigisthos gazed at the queen and a grim look settled on his face. "He wears a crown; he will always be on his guard."

# 5: THE JUDGEMENT OF PARIS

[*Chorus of elders*]
I
What insanity drove the Greeks to sail against
Troy? A thousand ships and fifty thousand men!
Half the principalities sent their warriors,
Leaving enough to man their walls, and those too old
Or too young for the expedition. Fewer than half,
A quarter, or a tenth, would return after many winters.
The others had listened to Atreus' sons: first Agamemnon
Commanding, then Menelaos pleading for support to punish
The violation of the Law of Hospitality—the
Abduction of Helen by the Trojans! Having listened,
They declined. Truth be told, they were wise.
Troy was a storied legend of wealth and power. No Greek
City had ever measured strength against Priam's walls,
Or even braved the blue-green seas to weigh the dangers
They would face. Brilliant Achilles agreed to go;
He sought his own glory for it had been foretold
That he alone could vanquish Hector, the doughty defender.
He scorned the oracle that tied his fate to this matchless deed.
He would not live long beyond this glorious moment,
Perfidious Paris, a mere archer, would fell this hero.

II
Insanity, the Judgment of Paris they called it, a divine jest
Was perhaps intended, but it brought tragedy.
Three goddesses, who should have known better, vied
For the golden apple inscribed "To the Most Fair."
And Paris the clueless presumed he could decide among
Goddesses which one should win this worthless prize.

So he chose Aphrodite, who promised the fairest woman—
Helen, Menelaos' wife—spurning wisdom and domestic
Bliss as promised by Athena and Hera respectively,
As bribes! Thus was set in motion events that would bring
Shame and pain, all the worst in gods and men.
The earth was young, gods and men still consorted;
Helen herself was said to have been sired by Zeus.
Who, insatiable, lusted also for Thetis, lively
Goddess of the sea, beloved of Hephaistos,
God of craft. But an oracle warned that any male offspring
Born to Thetis would eclipse his father. So Zeus
Chose for her brave but mortal Peleas whose son, Achilles,
By brilliant and heroic deeds would slay Hector and rip out
The heart of Troy's resistance and defense.
But to the wedding of Peleas and Thetis, Zeus decreed
That they not invite Eris, goddess of discord and strife.
He banished the nay-saying, disagreeable sprite,
Hoping to bring peace and harmony among the gods.
Would that it were so easily accomplished!
She cast into their midst that fateful apple of gold,
Of Discord, that goddesses should vie to be judged the Most Fair.

III
The "Judgment of Paris" would cause the Greeks much hurt.
It also broke the heart of the wood nymph whom Paris had
Seduced. She had tripped through the woods
On Mount Ida when a Trojan hunting party
Led by Paris wandered, lost and confused by the
Trails fashioned by elves and nymphs in mischief
Within the forest. Mother Ida's child fell o'erwhelmed
By the beauty of the Trojan prince and allowed
Him to catch a glimpse of her. He loved her then,
And often came to the sloped woods, until

Those three goddesses came shamelessly to seek his "Judgment."
Olympians though they were, they could not escape the malice
Of Eris, provoked by exclusion from the wedding. Forlorn
And joylessly did the wood nymph wander around the valleys
Near Troy. What of Menelaos, brave, prudent and loyal?
He was left to bay like a young wolf, wounded and lost,
Straining with every atom of his being and energy to find
The world he lost—Argos, Agamemnon, and Helen.
Did all-seeing Zeus or far-seeing immortal Apollo,
Zeus' son, think they could out-wit Eris by dismissing her?
Big mistake, to belittle the goddess. The gods were foolish,
The goddesses no less, Eris alone did not
Deserve the blame. Agamemnon too, with his
Compliant brother, might have stepped back from war.
Yet he slew his own daughter, first-born Iphigenia.

IV
Ambiguous are the auguries of the gods, O Greeks,
Gathered to sail against Troy! Two eagles, black and white,
Ripped a mother rabbit and her unborn twins. We thought
That foretold our victory, the rabbits' fate would be Troy's. But
The goddess of the hunt was angered by the cruelty
To the unborn twins, though some say Agamemnon or
His followers had slain a deer in her sacred forest.
Thus were Greek ships doomed to the roiling winds, the churning
Seas, and unwontedly dark skies. So Khalkhas the Seer
Inquired again: the sacrifice of a high-born virgin's life
Artemis demanded, he deemed, and at last Agamemnon slashed
Iphigenia's throat, spilt her life on the shore.
Ambiguous the morals of the gods. Some say that divine
Artemis substituted for the maiden a deer;
Others that she was transported to Tauris,
Human sacrifices there to perform for the goddess.

And yet others that brilliant Achilles defied Agamemnon
And saved Iphigenia, a lame and vain hope.
So sailed the fleet into the sparkling sea for battle against
Troy, whose plains were broad and horses many. Hector
The fair led their men. How long did the battle rage?

V
And how long did the wrath of Clytemnestra seethe?
Would she ever forgive her husband and her king,
Father of Orestes, Elektra, and Iphigenia?
She, a king's daughter, knew of course, how to rule,
But did not expect to do so, so soon or for so long.
And she brought to the royal bed, Aigisthos, cousin
To the king. More had long been whispered in the city
About their fathers, Atreus and his brother Thyestes.
But of the queen, the elders expected faithfulness to the king;
They did not, could not, conceive of anything else—
Their imagination could not see into a mother's
Heart or understand the fiery anger turned into cold
Fury unquenchable, sustained for ten winters.
Men, clueless of the dark passion that the queen could not
But hold in her heart, not willfully but still, a flood
That would not be held back or staunched, denied or lost.
And what would it bring in its train? Death and more blood,
To a house that already had shed more than its lot.
Aigisthos, alas, would also be embroiled, Thyestes'
Son, but beloved of Atreus and of Agamemnon.

# 6: AGAMEMNON'S DOOM

Who knows the heart of a king?

When the winds becalmed the Greek armada in Aulis, Agamemnon sacrificed his own daughter to appease the gods so the ships could sail for Troy. But of the hundred ships that sailed, only one now limped into Mycenae's harbor.

Many Greeks murmured that it was the king's obdurate lust for Chryseis that provoked divine pestilence against them and lengthened the war. When all the chieftains together persuaded him to return the war captive to her father, Agamemnon's prolonged the war by his next action. He took Achilles' war captive, Briseis, from that champion. As the latter sulked, the slaughter of the Greeks continued.

Now the king of Mycenae was back. He learned eight summers ago that his queen had taken Aigisthos as a lover. Agamemnon had returned with Cassandra as his latest war bride. What was on the king's mind?

On a brilliant early summer day, the entire city turned out to welcome their king. The trumpet fanfare was elaborate and triumphant, befitting a welcome for the conqueror of Troy. When the beacons flashed their message two moons ago, the queen and counselors prepared the royal city of Mycenae for the return of their king and his troops. Let the celebrations begin!

The games were a raucous success with the crowd that poured out of the houses of stone and mud. Smoke from a hundred bulls and sheep roasting wafted over the city in heady festivity and dispelled the stale, relentless tension built up over his absence for ten winters. The aroma of burned meat mixed with salt and garlic hung in the air and lured the city into the triumph. Crowds roared as the men wrestled. Then in groups and in single exercise, the warriors showed off their skill, maneuvering their spears before flinging them as a last flourish.

The populace watched with suspended breath as swordsmen slashed and stabbed. They observed with interest the elaborate demonstration of the latest in warfare, archery. Many fighting men deemed it less than honorable to kill someone unable to spit you in the eye or demand what kind of man it was come to challenge or kill him.

*Agamemnon, king of men! Hail, conqueror of Troy, master of Mycenae and Lord of the Argives.*

The king's dark curls were now flecked with grey, as was his well-trimmed beard. His face and arms bore the deep tan of those who labored for many summers on Troy's plains; even his thin lips, a feature inherited from his father Atreus, were tanned. His voice, whether in command or in debate, was gravelly as his father's had been, and like Atreus, he had the eyes of a candid man, frank and direct but without giving away any of his thoughts. He shared this trait of the eyes with his cousin Aigisthos.

A generation ago, Atreus had won the kingship of Mycenae. Now, Agamemnon himself had led an expedition of all Greeks that sacked Troy—a city known to most Greeks only through rumors of wealth and power. What further ambitions lurked in his restless heart?

#

While waiting to storm Troy, the king had spoken with Ulysses, Menelaos, and other Greek chieftains about planting a colony on the fertile Trojan plain. But they persuaded him it was foolish to stretch his rule so many leagues away from Mycenae. He then tried to interest them in assembling the soldiers in Greek states who had lost their chiefs and did not wish to serve new, untested princes.

"When we get back," he said as the embers smoldered by a late campfire, "I'd like to rally those left leaderless to see if we might not visit our wrath on those who held back from this expedition. What do you think?"

"If I live to see my wife and son again, I would fight by your side," declared Ulysses as he drained his wine goblet and prepared to leave for the night. "If I do not, I pray you ride to their support and muster those of my troops that remain—they would be proud to fight beside yours." Wily Ulysses was so full of schemes and unusual ideas that many of his fellow Greek chieftains were never sure of him, but Agamemnon was happy to take him at his word. He particularly liked Ulysses' scheme of leaving a large wooden horse as a 'gift' for the Trojans.

"Menelaos, what say you?" Agamemnon asked his younger brother as they stood up to retire. "Should we build a federation of Mycenae and as much of Greece as will join us?"

"Brother, we should wait until we are safe in Greece before dreaming of your next project."

"We've always plotted together," cried Agamemnon. "I need your caution, but also your support. The Trojans are defeated."

"But the seas are not," replied his stolid younger brother. "We should not tempt the gods. Safe in Mycenae or Sparta, I would plot and plan with you. You can always count on me."

#

The king wondered again now about the fate of his brother. Poseidon's storms had separated their ships on the voyage back from Troy. He hoped his brother was already in Sparta with Helen and getting reacquainted with his still lovely bride, who had provided the excuse for the expedition against Troy. But what if the sea prevailed against the ships? Who would help him with his next scheme? Menelaos had always been the first to support his plans, more cautious but always supportive.

His cousin Aigisthos had also always been part of his inner circle, but now he would face him as the queen's lover. His sister had reported several autumns since that Clytemnestra had sent Orestes and Elektra from Mycenae to live with her in Phocis. It did not surprise him. Everybody loved Aigisthos. And it was better that Clytemnestra took him to her bed instead of a commoner or even an aristocrat. But now he was back and the queen... The questions always went back to the queen.

How would he avoid quarreling with the queen, since the Trojan princess Cassandra his war trophy, accompanied him? She was carrying his child and her time was nearly due. Would the queen be jealous, perhaps angry? As he approached the palace, he saw a crowd had gathered by the steps.

"Hail Agamemnon, king of men!" The king waved. He recognized the counselors and the queen and many of the palace guards. Some counselors tottered and looked ready to retire; had they stayed out of some sense of obligation to see that the queen did not mishandle her responsibilities?

"Hail Agamemnon! Let your charioteer unfasten your sandals so you may walk up these steps by this royal walkway," cried Clytemnestra as she flung a woolen robe dyed in rich purple on the floor.

"What an extravagant idea," the kind declared, although he beamed. "I won't walk all over your handiwork, my queen. Such extravagance might provoke the good people of Mycenae."

"But you must," cried the queen. "My ladies and I have woven this from the best wool in the Argolid and dyed it with Phoenician treasure to celebrate your victory!"

"No, sire, it is a barbarian custom. It would attract the envy of the gods," spluttered one counselor. "Everything in moderation is our way."

"Why, Counselor," interjected the queen, "I did not think I would ever hear you speak. Were you not one of those who took a vow never to speak in my presence?"

The queen had planned the ceremony with the magnificent robe to welcome the victor of the Trojan War while many in the council had objected to the staggering cost. As the counselor mumbled, the queen turned again to the king. "Come, my lord. The celebration must be worthy of the deed. There is nothing that can compare with what you have achieved; we cannot laud and honor it with anything ordinary or customary. What do you think King Priam would have done if he had won?"

"Such extravagance," replied the Greek commander-in-chief, smiling with pride like a dog wagging his tail. "You were always one for the extravagant gesture."

"It's not more than you deserve."

Thus, the queen persuaded Agamemnon, as his charioteer removed his sandals to wash the king's feet. Palace maids poured the water and dried his feet before he walked on the purple. It was a magnificent carpet of the softest wool, dyed a color that evoked lilacs, violets, amethyst, and the deep stormy seas. This extravagant gift might also serve as a large shawl and cape or an elaborate robe. Maids followed the king and gathered up the lavish indulgence of the queen.

The royal party gathered in the throne room where the counselors paid their respects, and each received royal thanks for faithful service rendered during the king's absence. The queen's ladies had prepared wine and food that servants brought for their refreshment, though everyone understood that this was not a night for feasting. That would come later.

Tonight's ceremony would be a brief welcome. Commanders had dismissed the troops to their families or to the barracks. Heralds assured the city elders of the king's attention within the next day or two. Soon enough, everyone left the royal couple who retired to a cozy alcove by the banquet room. Agamemnon still had not decided how to broach the subject of Cassandra when the queen said,

"I understand you have a beautiful war trophy, from the royal family of Troy, who has the gift to see the future. What has she foreseen for Mycenae?"

"Oh, Cassandra," he replied. "She sometimes rambles and sometimes rants. Everyone says the gods have touched her and no one in Troy paid her any attention."

"Some compare her in beauty to Helen and even to the goddess Aphrodite."

"Well, she is exquisite with flowing red hair... very unusual. There are whispers that the god Apollo, no less, wooed her and hoped to gain her hand with that gift of sight you mentioned. She reminds me of Iphigenia, except for the hair color. Our daughter would have grown up to look like her. They would be about the same age."

Too late, Agamemnon realized in his rambling he had touched on a topic sure to inflame the queen's temper. "I hope you have stopped fussing about that matter," he stammered. "At least, I hope you would not still be resentful."

Clytemnestra fought to restrain the revulsion that brought gall and bitterness up to sting her throat and tears to her angry eyes. Pale as ice, she stared at him. Then she said, beginning in a whisper, "I am not *still* resentful of your foul deed..."

She crashed into a full-throated yell, "I will ALWAYS BE FURIOUS AT YOU!"

The silence that rang with the echoes of the queen's anger stunned Agamemnon into silence. She looked at him with glacial restraint, but injected venom into what she said next, "And the servants say she is with child."

"By the gods, you are well-informed."

"I ruled Mycenae for ten winters. Was I supposed to have done that blindfolded?"

"That might have been preferable for some counselors, I hear. Did they give you trouble?" asked the crafty king, trying now to distract the queen.

"Not more than I could handle," Clytemnestra replied, shaking her head to dismiss the king's bait. "But don't change the subject. It is a matter of bringing disgrace on your queen. I won't even bring up the despicable things you said about me to the men when you refused to return Chryseis, one of your earlier captives, to her father. Now, this Cassandra..."

"She shall be your slave even though she bears my child," Agamemnon conceded at once. He abandoned all his plans to move Cassandra into the royal bedroom or to an adjacent room when the queen revealed how well-informed she was. Now he pleaded, "Don't be so prim and proper."

"We are beyond that, Agamemnon," she replied from a place beyond emotion. "You've insulted me. It is an outlandish custom to have more than one wife. No doubt you learned too much of Priam and his fifty sons, and it all went to your head!"

"It is no more foreign than to trample over such a costly cloth as you laid out for me," cried the king. He pretended to laugh but was clawing like a man slipping down the side of a muddy hill as he tried to win his wife over or distract her.

"I did that to honor what you and the Greeks accomplished in Troy. What you did is an indignity to me and all Greek women," she replied with frost in her voice. "And if your trophy bears a boy, it will complicate matters for Prince Orestes."

"Well, you have not been so pure and proper yourself, you could not resist taking a lover," Agamemnon shouted. At this moment, he saw Aigisthos in the doorway and shouted out at him, "What kind of man are you to make love to your brother's wife?"

His face set as stone, Aigisthos looked the king in the eye as he walked in and said, "Hello, Cousin. What kind of man are you to expect your wife to live like a widow?"

The king smirked and said, as if they were soldiers sharing stories by a campfire, "You think men and women are alike in their needs and abilities, Brother? That is not our way."

"Not alike so much as entitled to equal respect as mothers of our children, I would say. The queen proved that while ruling in your absence, even though your last orders to the elders did not encourage them to support her."

"I only told them to delay decisions with consequences beyond two harvests," declared the king.

"Don't expect thanks for your statesmanship," replied his cousin.

"I assumed I would return soon. Who foresaw the war to last as long as it did?" complained Agamemnon as he sat and picked up his goblet of wine.

"A few elders took the view that such decisions included making repairs to our walls, digging new wells, or building improved roads. Others obstructed the will of a woman."

"I am confident the queen was more than equal to such silly views, since you were here to ease matters along as you always do," the king retorted. "You helped her with the council of elders, did you not?"

"Whenever I felt they needed me, which was seldom. You should appreciate your wife's capabilities."

The king accepted this rebuke with smiles and nods. Then he noticed Aigisthos wore a sword. He leaped out of his seat, drawing his own in a well-practiced instant. "You came ready to fight over this?"

"Only if it becomes necessary," replied the other, now drawing his sword. "Leave us, O Queen, and let the fates decide."

Clytemnestra withdrew, but her feet dragged and her face turned white.

"Are you challenging me? Have the gods robbed you of your senses? Are you so besotted by the queen as to champion her tired, old grief?" The king strode away from Aigisthos, swinging his sword from left to right and back.

His cousin paced away from him and glared as the silence thickened and then said in a faraway voice. "I fight to avenge my brothers."

"So, it was you who killed my father," cried Agamemnon as he struck at a small table, destroying it with a single blow.

"Do not pretend that is news to you. Surely you have not forgotten all the special training you ordered for me? A convenient lapse of memory? I don't think so," Aigisthos said before he had to parry a thrust from the king who dashed at him with his sword pointed at his heart.

Agamemnon followed that first exchange with a furious series of slashes from left and right in a tight figure-eight pattern. He spun often to gain speed for his slashing attacks. His cousin returned blow for blow while he searched for a weakness in the king's strokes. Soon the two men fought with heaving chests and loud grunts.

"Are you going to fight or talk?" shouted Agamemnon, continuing his attack. "You are lucky that I am not well rested."

"Making excuses already?" This remark provoked another flurry of angry strikes and thrusts from the goaded king.

Aigisthos was hard pressed to defend himself from this frenzied attack, even though he had trained daily. But the urgency of the best exercises failed to come up to the raw intensity he now faced in the attack of the leader of all the troops against Troy, who had fought for ten summers driven by the lust for slaughter and conquest. The commander-in-chief, the king—there was also a peculiar aura around these titles. Aigisthos fought not against an ordinary man, but against one who represented the authority of the city-state. Agamemnon had been the leader of a great federation of cities banded together on a mission, one that Zeus himself sanctioned. For ten summers, he led the Greeks as a dominant wolf led his pack, sleek, strong, and cruel.

Aigisthos on his part drew on the memory of his father's tale of what had happened to the brothers he never knew and how Atreus' hate and lust for vengeance had murdered them as he drove the king back with vicious thrusts and thunderous slashes of his own. "This is for the brothers I never knew. For my mother-sister that Atreus' cruelty drove my father to violate!"

"Perhaps you should have come with us, Aigisthos," cried the king applauding the skill and passion of his opponent. "You might have shortened the war for us, my Brother."

"Do not flatter me, Cousin. You could not have faced the daily reminder of Atreus' impious deed."

"Reminding me you have had your revenge of him is a mistake, Brother," the king yelled as he drove his cousin across the floor of the banquet room. There was more art and design in their swordplay now, as if they had learned each other's natural rhythms. As they approached the doorway, Aigisthos dodged a thrust and whirled around the king so they exchanged places and it was the king who now had his back to the door. The men clinched with their swords crossed in front of them and struggled until the king drew strength from yet another unknown reserve and pushed Aigisthos away.

"You will not end the House of Agamemnon tonight," cried the king.

"That House shall not end while Orestes lives, and he need not fear anything from me," shouted Aigisthos as the two men clinched their swords. Both struggled now with sweat dripping off their faces and heaving chests.

"What do you mean—the prince has nothing to fear from you?"

"Exactly that," replied Aigisthos, as he parried a sweeping slash by the king. "After I kill you, I shall send word to him he can come here to rule Mycenae whenever he likes."

"You are a bigger fool than I thought," said the king. "You'll never kill me, and if you do, my son will kill you!"

The king fought as one crazed, often making unnecessary sweeping and spinning moves, as if expecting attacks from other quarters. Twice, he pushed his opponent with his left shoulder as a warrior with a shield on that side might. In addition, the mantle of leadership, with all its attendant ceremonies, seemed to induce a joy in the acts of battle, of making a kill. Aigisthos fought as the leader of the dogs that defended against wolves, as one that had earned to the right to lead these lesser wolves. Against the bloodlust of the marauders, he battled with the devotion and desperation of the shepherds.

From the door, Clytemnestra appeared with the magnificent purple robe and flung it over the king's head. She escaped as he whirled around with his sword in a sweeping circle. Then, as the king paused with his sword in one hand raised high and the other hand reaching to remove the robe from over his head, she thrust fiercely. Her own broad dagger bore all the sorrow and anger she had carried for ten summers, struck at his armpit where sinews and blood vessels, nerves and bones met. The king gave a great cry, but tightening his right arm fast over his armpit, took his sword with his left hand, and charged at her.

"I remember how you change sword hands," cried his cousin, who stepped in between them without hesitation and clinched swords again with the king. "You taught me that," he said to taunt Agamemnon. "It must have been useful in Troy."

The swords rang again, though the king was in great pain and lost blood in thick spurts. He grew pale and slipped from time to time in his own gore. With a two-handed stroke, Aigisthos knocked the king's sword away to one side and swung his sword back to slice Agamemnon's throat. It cut through the windpipe and arteries by the neck so that the king died with a choked, gurgling sound.

A great cry came from the queen. Her face was pale and drawn, she grimaced as if in great pain. She howled as if delivering a child carried for ten times nine moons.

# 7: CASSANDRA

Soldiers marched to the plain but sturdy chariot that had followed Agamemnon's vehicle, ornate with well-worked bronze, and took Priam's daughter to her cell. It was in a part of the building that also housed the palace. But it had few torches and the sturdy walls here spelled not defiance against those who tried to enter but gloom and doom to those inside who looked to escape. The captive princess was heavy with child.

[*Cassandra's lament*]
This is an evil place;
It stinks like a slaughterhouse.
I smell the stains of foully murdered kin.
I see ghosts of children.
They are young boys who have not yet lost their milk teeth!
They skip and dance,
Laughing to one another.
They are caught and... and... butchered!
The murderer saved their hands, cut up and cooked their bodies.
Then his servants served the dish to their own father at a banquet—
What monsters lived here?

There, a young girl, approaching puberty.
Her breath is fresh, she steps lightly and her dark curls
Bob and tease the wind.
When she smiles, it is like the day breaking,
It is the end of winter. Magical spring awakens the buds
And the butterflies flit from flower to flower.

Bees hurry to collect the sweetness.
Aargh! What impious horror!
She is bound and gagged
And laid face down on a funeral bier.
Her throat is cut, and she bleeds—
For the gods, the pitiless gods...

It is Agamemnon, my lord and master—
I cannot believe this, but I must.
He who conquered Troy and took me for his trophy,
It was he who drew the knife and performed this ghastly deed.
How dare the gods demand, abide, the slaughter of one's own child?

Radiant Apollo, who came to me long ago to woo me with
This terrible gift, that I should hear and see the future.
I was too young then to bear this awe-full burden,
It was too heavy an office for my giddy head.
When I spurned you, your wicked spite doomed
What visions I had to go unheeded.
Why now do I see so clearly the past, that of my lord and master?
Aargh! I see you too—handsome, cruel, terrible, and all-seeing.
It was you who spoke through Kalkhas, the evil man who gave his soul
To be your mouthpiece.
I see him too, his skull on fire with
Your divine flame.
He glories in this, the miserable idiot.
Did you let him see the battles on the Trojan plains?
We had our seers too; they brought offerings to you and to
Zeus, without stinting on the lambs or the bulls.

Were Greek prayers and offerings better than ours?
Did our prayers not count for Hector's life?

O Apollo, why will you let me now die here,
With the child ripped from my womb?
I see the men come,
They will kill me
And slice the baby from my womb.
I wept for Hector, killed before the gates of Troy.
I wept for my father Priam
Who had to bury his sons and soldiers.
I mourn now the little boys
And that young girl.
I can weep no more.
But you, brilliant Apollo,
Have you betrayed Agamemnon, my lord and master,
In atonement for letting the Trojans die and our city
destroyed?

Aargh! Aargh! Aargh!
They have slain my Lord Agamemnon!
His own queen and his cousin have done the deed,
(Though it was difficult for them).
They have done this on his day of victory, in his own house—
The ghosts of the small boys and of the young girl rejoice;
I see them dance together,
The burden of their sorrows has been relieved.

They called me mad; that I am, for trying to understand the moods
Of the gods. You gave me sight to see what would come to pass,

I went mad trying to understand why; why our prayers and offerings
Made no difference. Why did you require them and accept them and then
Ignore our pleas anyway?
Insane are those who think you gods
Are fair and just and uphold the same principles you set for us!

Poor Orestes, I see Apollo will plague you with the noble ambition
To avenge your father and your king. You and your sister have grown strong
With your aunt, sister to my Lord Agamemnon, in Phocis,
(Even though it is a tiny village compared to Troy).
Your cousin Pylades escorts you through the woods,
Many are the birds and beasts that wander in them.
He leads you along secret paths among the rocks and dunes.
He has become your brilliant friend, for he loves you.
You, shining Apollo, will harass Orestes into killing Aigisthos.
But why drive him also to murder his own mother?
That is murder, most impious, monstrous, most foul.
Will you absolve him from that stain; can you—even you?
Though a stranger to me, Orestes, what I see of your future
Shrouds me in madness. Seeing what is in store for you
Who could remain sane?

The soldiers came late in the night to the cell where Cassandra lay tossing with her visions and nightmares. Her cell was clean and had small comforts like a jug of water and fresh straw. She lay in it with the scent of an Argive spring. It was not such as usually held thieves, bandits, robbers, or prisoners of conscience; those cells were always putrid and bare of all but lice and mice. Neither the queen nor Aigisthos desired to make this captive suffer. They only wanted her and her child put away.

The men were those who had followed the queen and Aigisthos for many summers while the king was away at war. One of them said, "It does not seem right to kill a woman of such beauty and so great with child."

The leader of the guards replied, "We are soldiers. We do not think or argue about right or wrong."

Another guard said, "But look at her, so pale, with hair so red as one never sees in Greece."

"Have someone has bewitched you?" asked the leader.

"Of course not," said the second guard. "But it is easier to kill in battle, even as Aigisthos killed the king in single combat. They fought for a long time, I hear. There was much slashing and clinching of swords."

"Hush! We will not speak of such things," declared their leader.

A third guard spoke up, "You are right. We may not talk about that. But someone will. It is difficult to conceal the absence of a victorious king on the day after we celebrate his return."

"Aigisthos will speak of that," replied the leader. "He has a way with words."

The first guard said, "I hear he did it to avenge his brothers whom the old king slew. Nobody imagines he was ambitious for the throne."

The second guard chimed in, "He has mistreated none of us, nor have I heard that he has taken advantage of the queen or anyone in the palace for pleasure or gain."

"All this may be true, but we are not here to discuss him or anything else," declared the leader.

"Yes, so what do we do now?" asked one guard.

"Take the captive out of here, and kill her and her child," said the leader.

"There will be a lot of blood," said the second guard.

"So there will be," the third.

"We are also to see that the bodies get a decent burial," said the leader.

"Burial? Who buries prisoners?" asked one guard.

"Orders from Lord Aigisthos," declared the leader.

# 8: THE KING IS DEAD

The vast stones of the great hall in the palace grew cold.

The queen shivered, not only because of the chill of the night but also because she struggled to maintain her composure. Agamemnon lay dead, and Aigisthos now ordered the captain of the palace guards to execute Cassandra and the child she was carrying. Then pale, tense, and trembling, the queen hurried to the royal chamber like a mare gathering her foals away from the scent of wolves. As she whirled around and left in haste, the torches flickered.

Her lover saw the doubt in the brave captain's eyes and reassured the man with a nod. The captain did not relish his task, but he had already heard murmurs in the alleys of the city — grief, resentment, and sheer anger — against the Trojan war-bride. People in the city had lost ninety-nine out of every hundred men who had sailed to war against Troy. Their murmurs against Agamemnon buzzed like angry bees. If he had lived, the king might not have been able to protect Cassandra. Aigisthos and the captain left the throne room to carry out their separate burdens. One would execute a war trophy laden with child. The other went to comfort a woman he loved, who did not deserve to face this world of sin and sorrow, of murder and vengeance.

"I had to do it," said the queen without looking up as Aigisthos entered their chamber. "Killing Agamemnon was easier, I'm sorry to say. He is the father of my children, but he might as well have killed me when he slaughtered Iphigenia. I feel sorry for Cassandra, but she reminded me too much of the man who killed Iphigenia."

She burst into sobs of rage, "What a brute he was to say that girl reminded him of our daughter!"

Aigisthos embraced her and said nothing. Her neck and shoulders were as tight as the strings of Orpheus lyre as he entered Hades, where Eurydice was a prisoner.

"You say we always have a choice. Do you think I made the wrong one?"

"Only the gods would dare answer yes or no, but since you have already taken action, I say you should not torture yourself further." He held the queen to comfort and protect her in his arms as she wept her heart out in grief yet again for her first-born. She mourned also for Cassandra, and even for Agamemnon.

The maids came to take away the torches, leaving only a small one for the couple to sleep with. Still, Aigisthos held the queen. As the little torch flickered its last moments, he felt her tension ease. He ran the tips of his fingers like feathers over her bare arms. Her sobs subsided as the tensions of the doom-laden events of the day eased out of her tight neck and shoulders. She purred as arousal of a different passion took hold of her, and they glided to bed.

#

While it was yet dark, before the hour for the roosters to crow, the queen awoke from the chill of being left alone. She took comfort from the candle that Aigisthos had left lit on his side of the bed. It was burning low, signaling he had been up for a while. She saw him at the window, looking into the night. She asked, "Do you see anything helpful?"

The queen drew on a light cloak over her night-dress and approached her lover, who smiled and declared, "I see what we must do today."

"We must convene a council of the elders and tell them everything," said the queen.

"Yes. We would not want to rule without their consent, would we?"

"You were always more generous about their contributions than I, but I know we will not get away with behaving like Agamemnon. How did he do the things he did?" she asked, frustrated and bemused.

"My cousin was a shrewd man, but more important than that, he *won* the battles into which he led the city. A victor gets wide latitude, even if there are more widows to mourn those killed in his service. Despite our celebrations yesterday, however, I think the city does not consider the outcome of the war against Troy a victory. The people feel hollow. As I walked through the town yesterday, I felt a sense of devastation rather than celebration."

"What will you tell the elders?"

"That I killed Agamemnon and intend to marry you," Aigisthos said, looking up at the queen. "That we both agree to leave whenever

Orestes comes to claim the throne. We still agree on these matters, I trust."

"Yes," said the queen. "I would not have left Agamemnon alive, you know. But I am content to leave the throne for Orestes.

The sun soon made its way clear of the cypresses on the eastern hills, and Aigisthos sent messengers to inform the elders that the council would meet.

"What did you think when our affair began?" asked Clytemnestra, stabbed by doubt and overwhelmed by the enormity of their actions.

He beamed as he recalled the personal moment, the night the queen admitted him into her bed-chamber. "I thought it was pure heaven. What troubles you?"

"The Greeks might have returned that year," she said, shaking her head. "We would have had to face the decision about Agamemnon then."

"They might never have returned at all," replied her lover. "I did not wish that upon our men and heroes, but I left that to the gods. Whether our love would last one month or forever was in Zeus' hands or in no one's."

#

"Honored Counselors," announced Aigisthos, a little later when the sun was high, his voice firm, yet friendly. "The king is dead."

Chaotic, confused outcries greeted this bald statement. The counselors all looked around the marbled chamber with the feigned nonchalance of cats, Hecate's inscrutable creatures. They peered to see if there were soldiers in attendance. Every one of them was a prudent man; they had each lived longer and accumulated more wealth than the average citizen.

Aigisthos knew the elders in many Greek cities feared a military tyranny and had persuaded the queen that they should not begin their reign with the show of force. It sufficed to know that the captain of the guards remained loyal and, for this meeting, would be within shouting distance but not visible from the chamber. Out among the trees within the city walls, the guards were on full alert even as the bright and fast warming sun cast a lazy haze in the sky. Bees buzzed as they went about their summer chores, and the occasional gusts of wind brought the scent of eucalyptus into the hall of wisdom.

"How did he die?" shouted several voices, with increasing confidence. Silence grew in the space of a breath, slowly exhaled.

"I killed him," declared Aigisthos. He paused among the buzz and added, "He fought and died well."

"Why?" challenged several voices.

"You are all old enough to understand why. I only learned of the reasons for the murderous hate within the House of Pelops when I was twenty. My father, Thyestes, demanded a terrible vow from me then. Those of you who knew him, have more knowledge of the story than I." Looking around, Aigisthos noticed hesitation within the muttering of the elders and that one of them was frowning. "Elder Aristides, is there something you wish to say?"

"My Lord Aigisthos, regardless of the feud between your father and old king Atreus, killing Agamemnon—regicide—is a serious crime. We must appease the gods."

Aigisthos thought about the speaker and his statement. It was a brave speech from an honest man, one who had gained his respect as he observed whenever he sat with or for the queen in the council. Lean and tall, Aristides wore his beard more carefully trimmed than most others in the council. His speeches were as skillfully presented. Hence Aigisthos elaborated, "We are seeking counsel from the temple and seers even now and will obey their oracles."

"Did you do this at the queen's bidding?" demanded several counselors.

"Elders, you all know the queen has never forgiven the king for the sacrifice of her daughter, their first-born Iphigenia."

"It was the will of Zeus that the Greeks should sail against Troy," asserted one of the well-perfumed elders. Several others whispered their agreement, signifying their disapproval of the queen's feelings.

"Yet it was the goddess Artemis who thwarted our ships," interjected another elder in a crotchety voice and contrary manner, prompting more grumbling.

"I do not understand the motives of the gods and goddesses," remarked Aigisthos. "But elders, let me ask those of you who have lost a daughter—was it only their mothers who mourned?" He paused before asking again, "If any has had the tragedy of a daughter violated, would there be even a moment's hesitation to avenge her honor?" The murmurs grew silent. Aigisthos paused again before saying,

"The queen wanted to do this, but I told her my reason was more pressing: the vow I made to my father twenty summers ago." Aigisthos shuddered as if he recalled that moment, then continued, "I waited for a suitable moment to fulfill that oath. There was always one more project for Mycenae to put me off. After the Trojans came and left with Helen, it was the wrong time to kill Agamemnon before he left; I had to do it as soon as he returned."

"Prince Orestes may not agree with all that the seers see or with what you have done," cried out another of the elders.

"That may well be, but the queen and I have decided on a path that we must take until it leads to a fork. I intend to marry her at the earliest propitious moment and we will send a message to the prince that whenever he wishes to claim his birthright, we shall leave."

"Leave Mycenae?" demanded a chorus of elders accustomed to the wealth and power of the royal city and its mighty walls.

"Yes. We hope, however, that until he arrives, we will have your counsel on matters regarding the Argolid. What do you advise regarding an announcement to the people?" Since he knew Agamemnon had never asked for advice, Aigisthos added, "I believe it is best to tell them what I have just told you. Do you agree?"

None of the elders put forward an alternative announcement, not even those who criticized what he proposed. Some wondered if they could announce the king's death later, but they could not agree on a date. The elders would procrastinate, he suspected, as he himself had done over fulfilling his vow.

"Who will go on the mission to bring this news to Orestes?" asked a practical counselor.

"He and his sister are with their aunt, are they not?" asked another.

"Yes, they have been in Phocis for the past seven winters. On horseback, it is a ten-day journey from Mycenae," replied Aigisthos. No one volunteered, so he asked Aristides, who agreed.

"Are you acquainted with Strophios and with the way there? How large an escort do you want?"

"Well, I fear nothing from the King of Phocis, whom I have met once or twice, and the way to his city is not dangerous although it is not a comfortable ride," replied the tall slim counselor. "Can you send two or three men to accompany us? I will bring a slave to help with making camp along the way."

"We will do as you see fit. I shall ask the captain of the guards to send a herald and one of his trusted men. Make ready to leave by the third sunrise if you can."

"Are there any special instructions?" Aristides asked with his eyebrows raised and gesturing around the council of elders.

"Nothing other than what I have told you and will tell the people when we gather them. You may tell King Strophios and Orestes your own opinion of the state of affairs in Mycenae—I do not presume to ask you to tell us all what you think."

Aigisthos then addressed the elders for the last time that day. "Honored elders, may I ask that you please speak with your household and guests and tell them we shall today address the people of Mycenae? Let the people gather at noon in front of the palace. Our thanks to you all."

Some elders remained crowded around Aigisthos. They had all known about the queen's lover and knew well the man they had long considered Atreus' adopted son. Many times during the ten winters of Clytemnestra's regency, some had brought to his attention a command or order to which they objected. Aigisthos had sometimes deflected the command. He always left the elders with the sense that he understood their concerns and would give their views due consideration.

A few winters ago, some of them had approached him to protest expenditure from the city treasury to purchase purple dye from the Phoenicians, an essential part of the queen's gift to the king.

"It is an outrageous custom and so expensive," cried an elder.

"Not so expensive as it would have been if the queen did not contribute half of its cost, Counselor," observed Aigisthos.

"She had no right to use her bride price; that belongs to the king."

"She paid her share not from the bride price but from her mother's bequest."

"Then she did not contribute enough. I have heard what the queen mother's gifts amounted to."

"She could not use all of it."

"Why not?"

"Counselor, you are well-informed. You must know the gift was to two sisters and our queen could only keep half."

"You mean the queen withheld Helen's portion?"

"Yes, she continues to hope that Menelaos and Helen will soon be safe in Sparta."

"That woman has no right to anything Greek!"

"Good Elder, it is not for us to judge. If Menelaos forgives Helen, we should do the same." Aigisthos struggled to maintain his affability in some of these discussions.

Now, in the wake of the news about the king's death, certain elders pressed for special favors for themselves or their sons; a few said they were ready to retire and wished to recommend their replacements. As Aigisthos listened to each elder, he transfixed them with a frank and solemn gaze as if judging the dead like King Minos and his brothers, as they all believed. Some counselors grumbled that having someone who listened so intently tired them.

He paid most attention to Aristides and one or two others who had been most willing to serve the queen. Around them, he would rebuild a new council.

The queen who remained secluded in the royal chambers, had not opposed the proposal regarding Orestes when Aigisthos first mentioned it. But she asked if it was not a mistake to promise so publicly and so soon the abdication of the throne of Mycenae to her son. There could be no going back now. The news surprised the crowd while the elders, despite what they heard earlier, did not readily believe such a promise. Aigisthos knew that this was not the way usurpers proceeded, and for the time being, they regarded him as a usurper.

#

That night, the old watchman remained in the comfort of his own home, enjoying the familiar presence of his wife and his grandchildren before their mothers arrived to take the youngsters to bed. He had told the captain of the guards he would remain as watchman until King Agamemnon returned victorious. Honor and duty bound him to fulfil this duty. But he would not stay a day longer on the city walls; he intended to enjoy his retirement. He did not even miss the excitement the games had brought that day.

When Aigisthos spoke with the captain of the guards about the mission, however, he had the watchman in mind and said, "It would be helpful for the mission to include a familiar face at least. Who among the guards has met Orestes?"

"Most of the older men know of him. No one knows him well."

"What about the old night watchman?"

"Ah, you mean the old captain of the guards."

"Yes."

"He has just retired. He asked to retire yesterday, the day Agamemnon returned."

"Could we persuade him to go on one last mission for Mycenae? It will be more agreeable to Orestes and Elektra when they receive the news to see someone they grew up with. Their aunt Anaxibia will remember him. All this would ease Elder Aristides' mission."

"Yes, you're right," agreed the current captain of the guards, one of the few mature guards left behind when the fleet sailed for Troy. "He is familiar to them all. I think we might persuade the old watchman. Who else should go?"

"What do you suggest, Captain? I doubt we need a large escort for the mission."

"I would send the sword-master who trains the recruits. He's a sturdy fellow and one of our best soldiers. The watchman is still formidable with his spear, and the herald is ahead of his peers in sword practice so he can be an additional man at arms. I agree we have nothing to fear from King Strophios or the few bandits along the way. There are many mountains and hills before and after Corinth and more when they have to cross the Parnassus range near Phocis. The party will be on horseback for nine or ten hard days, but there will be no danger."

"Perhaps a small company should escort the party for a day's ride out," suggested Aigisthos.

"That too is a good idea; we could also send it back out in twenty days to await the return of the mission."

"We owe it to Counselor Aristides to do that much."

"Very well, sir. I'll make the arrangements."

Aigisthos stood but did not dismiss the captain of the guards. "Are the people restless?"

"Yes, but it will pass."

"From what I have heard, it was like this when news of Atreus' banquet for my father became known." The two men stood in grim silence. Neither of them was old enough to have direct knowledge, but they both had heard the whispers. "Our customs do not encourage anyone to oppose violence or even wrongdoing."

"But they exhort family members, sons, to vengeance," said the captain. Aigisthos sighed.

"When and where will this end?"

# 9: THE MISSION TO PHOCIS

They rode in the morning and in the late afternoon every day, stopping wherever they found shade to rest. Ten days of riding through the mountains that bound the Peloponnesus to the north of Greece brought the party from Mycenae to Phocis. It was the middle of a bright summer day when they interrupted the activities of the young royals.

"Orestes," called out a slim, tanned, and bewitching young girl with black curly hair as she interrupted two young men at sword practice. "We have visitors from Mycenae."

"This is not an excuse to escape your household chores, is it Elektra?" asked her brother. He had similar hair, inherited from both their mother and father, and was taller than his sister by a head. His blue-grey eyes gazed frankly and promised friendship while his sister's eyes sparkled like any lively young girl's, ready for adventure.

"We promised we would call you when we are ready for the archery lessons," recalled Pylades, whose hair was a dark brown with highlights of red like his father's. Younger than his cousin by a summer and a winter, he was as tall and as sturdily muscled. His confident bearing, however, commanded attention more than Orestes. "Did you not trust us?"

"You boys are impossible! The visitors are with the king. I saw them go into the palace. The watchman is with them. Do you remember him, Orestes?"

"Yes!" her brother answered, glad for news of a familiar personality. "I even recall when he was captain of the guards. He would ride with me sometimes and show me around Mycenae and Argos. He told me how disappointed he was not to go on the war with father."

"Perhaps he has news of our father... remember him?"

"I do, though he's been in Troy more than half my life," replied Orestes.

"The picture of him in my mind is not at all clear," remarked Elektra, frowning as if thwarted in her search for a favorite tunic not in its place among her clothes. "I can remember that terrible thing he did to Iphigenia and how mother cried and mourned."

"I remember that too," said the prince of Mycenae after a slight pause. "It is a painful memory that was fading. I wish you had not mentioned it."

"He did not visit us before the ships sailed for Troy," said Pylades, "so I never met him. The queen has been here several times. I think my mother likes her better than she does her own brother. At least I don't remember hearing mother talking about the high king of Mycenae."

"The high king of Mycenae has many worries that keep him away," Orestes said.

"You won't be like that when you become king, will you?" asked his cousin.

"I have never thought of becoming king," said the Mycenaean prince, surprised at the thought.

"I shall be king of Phocis someday. My father has told me that many times," declared Pylades, strutting up and down, waving his arms as if in receipt of adulation from a crowd.

At this, Elektra turned aside until she regained control over her composure. Orestes noticed her blush. With a sly grin, he leaned over and whispered to ask his sister if she imagined herself someday queen of Phocis, wife to Pylades.

#

The next day, the blue of the late summer sky was of such piercing clarity and depth as might have brought tears to one's eyes. Aristides gave thanks to the gods for such clear weather as he walked along the columned walkway on the east side of the palace to Strophios' chambers. He was a straightforward counselor with a mission from the new king of Mycenae.

Twenty summers ago, old King Atreus had given his only daughter in marriage to a strapping young prince in whom he saw something of himself. But though Strophios inherited the throne from his father not long after the wedding and somewhat resembled Atreus, he lacked the driving ambition that seemed peculiar to the House of Atreus. He declined to join the war against Troy, preferring the comfort of his isolated kingdom.

His queen had, after a few anxious years of marriage, given birth to a son, Pylades. The king of Phocis had been glad when Clytemnestra sent Orestes and Elektra to stay with them, happy to help and so that his prince would have playmates other than stable boys and chambermaids.

They were both happy also for Clytemnestra, for they understood the reason she sent the children to their keeping. Anaxibia felt obliged to send word to her oldest brother since Agamemnon was sure to find out about Aigisthos, and her silence would be awkward to explain.

Aristides and the king now walked about the palace gardens and the latter asked, "So what's the news of Agamemnon? Did he and his ships not return? That would be a disaster!"

Aristides replied, "The king of Mycenae has returned, but with only one ship."

"Out of a hundred?" interjected Strophios. "That is almost worse."

"And he only enjoyed one day of triumph. He is dead."

The king as his eyes narrowed and his lips pursed. "So, Clytemnestra killed him." Aristides looked up, and Strophios continued, "She had sworn to Anaxibia that she would. They were both inconsolable after the sacrifice... Iphigenia... before the fleet sailed off."

Aristides took this in and then said in measured tones, "It was Aigisthos who killed the king."

"Ah."

"Because of the feud between their fathers; that was what he told the council, and I for one do not doubt him," continued Aristides. "All the Mycenaean elders knew something about that feud, and most of them believe him. He says, however, to tell Orestes that whenever he is ready for the throne, it will be his with no fuss."

"He and Clytemnestra would leave Mycenae?" asked Strophios. "Do you believe him?"

Aristides sighed. "He told me I could tell you my opinion on the events. Yes, I believe he would. I also believe that he killed the king because of his vow to his father, Thyestes, as he said. He spoke to the council of elders and told us something of the fight with his cousin the king and about how he intended to marry the queen."

"I've only met him once when he accompanied the children here to live with us," remarked the king. "I think he is a... complicated man."

"Supposedly, he loved the queen even before her marriage to Agamemnon," said the counselor.

"I cannot imagine a man waiting for thirteen summers to possess the woman he loves."

"Fourteen," interjected Aristides. "He did not move into the royal chambers until after the summer following that in which the fleet sailed."

Strophios listened as Aristides continued to speak of his mission, but only smiled when Aristides repeated Aigisthos' promise that Orestes could return any time he felt ready to take over the kingship of Mycenae and the Argolid. After a pause, the host declared, "Orestes might want to do so after my son Pylades becomes king here in Phocis. That will not be for several years."

To the question in Aristides' gaze, he responded with thought and care. "I will not ride with him on that journey, if he makes it. Aigisthos has wronged none of us, and I shall speak for my wife and say that she preferred the company of her brother's wife to that of her brother."

Aristides nodded and, to change the subject, asked, "This city of yours in the hills is such a paradise; is there anything that troubles you?"

"Nothing that keeps me up at night," replied the king with a laugh. "But I worry about the rise of rival cults devoted to Dionysius and Apollo nearby." He paced in a circle and faced the elder.

"Ah, we saw Kalkhas, the seer devoted to Apollo, on our journey here," offered Aristides as he stretched his arms out. "He was far away from us, so we did not hail him. Besides, he walked with such purpose and urgency we felt it would have been an intrusion."

"The followers of Apollo are building a colony near Delphi," said the king, waving his hand towards the sun. "According to those who profess to know about such things, it is a place that has a sacred aura. They want to train seers there and establish the worship of Apollo. I am a little concerned as the followers of Dionysius have also chosen to establish themselves not more than a few thousand paces away."

"It is well that you are informed of their activities."

Strophios nodded to acknowledge the compliment and said, "Both communities profess openness in their intentions and their activities. I am inclined to let them be, so long as their zeal does not turn into hate or violence."

"Who are their followers?"

"Dionysius' followers are almost all from the vineyards. We all know him as the god of wine. The followers of Apollo are a very mixed group, but most of them are the serious, meditative type. I am sure there are people who can make sense of the different beliefs. I just keep myself informed of what they do."

"You have those who report to you among the communities?"

"My task is easier with the followers of Dionysius. There are members of the families of my guards who are members, and they bring regular reports. Besides, there is much gossip about their revels and merry making. Among the community of Apollo followers, there is less loose talk. I had to send two families to join them and get information that way."

The king looked at Aristides and they both shrugged. To change the subject, the Mycenaean elder asked the king, "How have the young people occupied themselves these days?"

"Pylades is trying to get the others interested in a new project—archery."

"Really? Our soldiers do not value that weapon, but..."

"I learned the other day that the Minoans in Crete have practiced it for hundreds of years. Some Trojans have become expert I hear," said the king.

"Is it effective?" asked the counselor.

"People say that a good archer is deadly at thirty-five paces and a very good one at twice that. It depends, of course, on the bow, and whether there is any wind, and if the target is moving."

"Can it penetrate armor or a shield?"

"Not well-made bronze armor or shields, I understand, but arrows can hurt a man in the legs and necks."

"Who makes the bows and arrows for you?"

The king squinted at Aristides as if sizing him up for an ulterior motive; the counselor from Mycenae shifted his feet and coughed. Then the king said, "A runaway slave from Thessaly, to the north of us. He does not speak Greek well. I would guess that some adventurous trader captured him from one of the barbarian tribes further to the north."

"That is the hard part of archery I imagine," remarked Aristides, "making the bows and arrows."

His host shrugged and said, "It seems to have taken the young people a fair bit of practice. They have been at it the whole summer; Elektra is the only one who can consistently hit the target at thirty-five paces."

"Good for her!" cried Aristides.

"Few fathers would think so," said the king, her uncle, looking at the counselor whose face remained neutral.

"How do the young men fare at it?"

"Pylades is not good at all. The sword is going to be his weapon of choice," said the king. "But Orestes could be good if he applied himself."

"Is he distracted?"

"I think he wishes he could be a better swordsman. It disappoints him that Pylades is so much better at it than he is; he wants to be more like my son."

"Mycenae looks up to Phocis."

"Yes, even though Orestes is older by a winter or so. Speaking of which, we have a special meal tomorrow night, to celebrate the second moon after the summer solstice. I was born fifty-three summers before that. Your party will stay at least through that evening, I hope."

"Thank you. I was born fifty-three springs ago, close to the equinox."

#

The watchman, meanwhile, spent his day delivering the gifts from Clytemnestra to her sister-in-law. He also handed to Orestes, with solemnity, the sword of his father, Agamemnon. "There are many stories told of this sword, Orestes. You can wear it with pride." The watchman also spoke of the events in Mycenae and of Aigisthos' offer to leave its throne whenever the young prince wished to return.

Prince Orestes shuddered, his face dark but blank. He stole a glance at his cousin and licked his lips, but said nothing. Electra, the Mycenaean princess, flushed and frowned as if trying to recall memories the waves and sand had buried too deeply.

Anaxibia, their aunt, was not at all stirred by the death of her brother.

"Aigisthos was the one who had been most respectful to my mother, Aerope," she said when the servants brought her the news. "He was the only male in the family to mourn at the queen mother's funeral." She wiped away her tears, and then continued, "Besides, how could I forget Iphigenia? I helped Clytemnestra nurse and wean her, and I was not less devastated when my brother sacrificed her."

The young prince, his sister, and their cousin were awestruck, however, by the sword itself. This was the sword that conquered Troy. The sight of it made Orestes eager to put more heart into his sword practice. The visitor from Mycenae smiled at the young people and said, "You give this sword the respect it deserves."

Pylades soon led the others in showing the watchman their archery grounds. Elektra beamed with delight at the old man's admiration for her skill. Goaded by this recognition of his sister, Orestes put more concentration and application into his arrows and shot almost as well. Pylades laughed off the invitation for him to show his abilities. Then, when it came time to show off their skills in swordsmanship to the watchman, he changed the program to riding knowing Orestes would do better at this. Elektra excused herself from this portion of the schedule of events, leaving to see if her aunt might need her help with preparations for the evening meal.

The next day, the king invited Aristides together with the herald and the sword-master to tour the palace and inspect the guards. Meanwhile, the watchman observed the young people at more of their exercises and reminisced with Anaxibia. "Oh, Captain," she cried. "Has it been twenty winters since you rode with us here?"

"I have not kept count, my lady, but that sounds about right," he replied. "I was proud and happy when your father picked me to ride with the small band that accompanied you and Strophios here after your wedding in Mycenae."

The feast for Strophios birthday was full of merriment and entertainment arranged by the maids and the palace guards.

Homeward bound, the party from Mycenae encountered no surprises on its journey homeward. An escort sent to meet them arrived in time to provide a guard for their last night and day on the road. The late summer heat led the travelers to ride in the mornings and evenings. Seeing Orestes and Elektra again gladdened the watchman, but he was as happy to retire from his last mission.

#

When the first rains of autumn arrived and one night the old watchman had a visitor at his small stone house. After a knock, a man entered his house and greeted him. "Good evening, Captain."

"It has been over twelve summers since anyone called me that," he replied.

"That is what you will always be to me," declared Aigisthos, taking off his hooded cape. "Forgive me for bringing some rain in with me." He raised a hand to signal to the old man he should remain seated. "I only came to thank you for undertaking that last mission."

"You are good to visit me, O King," said the watchman as he pointed to a tripod of staves to suggest that the king might hang his cape on it. The king declined with a polite shake of his head and shrug.

"I am used to holding my clothes or eating while on my feet, Captain," he said recalling life on the march with the older man.

"I am confident," replied the watchman, "that elder Aristides gave you a complete and faithful account of all that happened. For myself, I will add only that Orestes is not ready to return for the kingship."

"What did you think of the young prince?"

The old man paused before saying, "He loves Pylades and cares little about soldiering or ruling."

"I hope the love is returned," remarked the king.

"With the prince of Phocis, it is different, but he loves Orestes."

Aigisthos nodded and thought, *the prince will, when the time comes, become king and marry, and his life would be too full to include Orestes.*

"Pylades has led the others in taking up archery," said the watchman.

"So Aristides told me."

"Elektra is the best of them, only by a little, but it pleases her," opined the old man. "Orestes is good at it too. Pylades the ring-leader does not do so well, but he is a superb swordsman. Orestes lacks interest in that, but perhaps his new sword will inspire him."

"The king and queen of Phocis did us a great favor when they took in Orestes and Elektra," said Aigisthos. "I thought

Elektra, in particular, would be happier away from the palace here—with or without my coming. It was hard for her, growing up in Iphigenia's shadow and with her ghost."

"The aunt and uncle love the children of Agamemnon and treat them well. The children can stay for as long as they wish; they seem happy there too. Elektra has become more like her father, strong-minded and commanding." The old man paused before continuing, "She is, however, more restrained and recognizes the limits of her sex. Both of them love their cousin Pylades."

"The queen and I must stay here a little longer, then."

"Are you eager to leave, my lord?" the old captain ventured to ask.

"I fear that this will not end well when it ends," Aigisthos said. The retired watchman nodded. His thoughts on the matter saddened him. He voiced them.

"Yes. The people will accept you; the counselors-elders will accept you as their king. Anaxibia will accept you as king of Mycenae, even though you killed her brother. Perhaps Menelaos will also, whenever he returns. Even Orestes may accept you, for he does not seem to be the vengeful type." He and the king exchanged looks as those who have marched together against enemies learn and train to do. Then he continued,

"But who knows about the gods?"

"There are many things beyond our understanding or control," Aigisthos murmured. "Be well, Captain, and enjoy your grandchildren. If you have any need, just send me word."

"Thank you, my lord."

# 10: ORESTES' DREAMS

Seven winters after the death of Agamemnon in Mycenae, Orestes' nightmares began. In a room in the palace where he shared a bed with his cousin, he moaned as his head pounded.

[*Orestes*]
Dark, it was dark. Very dark.
I could see no glimmer of light.
No pain. No sensation of any kind.
In time, I sensed a sound. Whoosh-pound,
All-enveloping, it penetrated my being.
It was steady. Whoosh-pound, whoosh-pound.
The dark was an absolute absence
Of light. But I felt safe. Whoosh-pound.
It was impossible to tell how long
This lasted. Whoosh-pound.

After a long while, I became conscious of
A new sound, patter-patter-plop,
Patter-plop, patter-boom.
Faint, barely felt—not heard.
Patter-plop, patter-boom;
It grew stronger, I felt it more.
There was still the whoosh-pound
But the patter-boom was more frequent
And it grew stronger and stronger.

Patter-patter-boom, patter-boom.
Stronger still it grew.
Then I sensed it confined me.
Whoosh-pound, patter-boom.
But I could not move or see.

Whoosh-pound, whoosh-pound.
That became more urgent. I felt
Its intensity. The smaller sound also
Became more demanding. The dark became
More confining, more constricting.

Where is the light, any of it?

Whoosh-pound, patter-boom,
Again and again, and again, and again.
The darkness pressed on me as the sounds
Came faster and became more urgent.
The dark was desperate, so was I.
Desperation turned into panic as the darkness
Crowded in, leaned on me. I struggled
Against the dark, I didn't know where
Or how I was confined. Panic, fear—
But the dark was not a place to stay.
It closed further, pressed closer in on me.
Whoosh-pound, whoosh-pound,
Patter-patter-boom, patter-boom,
Panic, fear; fear, panic.

Harder and harder, the dark pushed in on me;
Where could I go?
Whoosh-pound, whoosh-pound, patter-boom
Patter-boom, patter-boom!
Panic! Fear!
Whoosh-pound, whoosh-pound, whoosh-pound!
Patter-boom, patter-boom.
The dark pushed by me. I kept my eyes closed
But I could see light. Light!
And pain! I screamed, I yelled.

Did anything, anyone, hear me?
Patter-boom, patter-patter-boom.
I screamed and cried and cried.

Patter-boom, patter-boom, faint
Then more loud, patter-boom, beat, patter-boom.
I could move! My eyes remained closed.
It was bright, I could tell.
Again I screamed and cried.
Something soft came into my mouth.
A new sensation! But it satisfied me.
Patter boom, patter boom.
How much time has passed?
Something soft in my mouth.
I opened my eyes; too bright.
Slowly shadows formed, and I saw a face,
A smile of such beauty and love.
The face came nearer, and I could see
It had eyes. Reflected in the eyes, I saw—
A viper. Screams! Again no sound,
How did I know there were screams?
Patter boom. Patter-patter-boom.
I saw the complete face screaming, but I heard no sound.
There was such anguish, anger, pain.
I did NOT feel safe.

Then the face dissolves. The smile is no more.
Instead, a skull appears, flames spring out of its eye sockets
And a ghastly sound echoes in my head.
Light, such as pierces the eyes to see, bursts
All around my skull,
Together with heat like a blast from the underworld.
Aargh! The light and the pounding in my head hurt.

Patter-boom, patter-patter-BOOM.
Panic, fear, pain.
It is a god—
Apollo appears in all his glory;
In my bones, I knew it was he;
There is no mistaking who it is—
Light of the sun and heat of the underworld.
He is angry. He screams about VENGEANCE.
The sound bounces around the inside of my skull.
I thrash and cry, and I feel
The sound reverberate—aargh! Aargh! Aargh!

"Orestes, wake up," Pylades cried. "You're having another nightmare!"

"Oh, my head hurts," Orestes moaned. "Hold me, please." Pylades stretched beside his lover, their bodies entwined.

"This is the third night in a row this week!"

"Are you keeping count?"

"I can't help it. You wake me up."

"I am sorry."

"You need to make them stop," declared Pylades.

"I know what Apollo wants," said Orestes.

"Then do it and end these nightmares."

"But I can't." Misery and frustration strangled Orestes' voice.

"Why not?"

"Because he wants me to kill my mother!"

"Unbelievable." Pylades still couldn't believe it, although they had discussed the dream when it first came weeks ago. He held his lover closer as if afraid to lose him.

"Yes," mumbled Orestes.

"But it was Aigisthos who killed your father."

"I can't argue with a god who does not stay to listen to my questions or protests."

"You are sure he wants you to kill your mother?" demanded his cousin for the tenth or twentieth time.

"I told you," was the weary reply. "He shows her to me in my nightmares. I am the viper she gives birth to and I bite her."

"That's... more than strange."

"I wouldn't mind if my head didn't hurt so much."

"You are silly."

"But I love you," declared Orestes, "more than I love Elektra or can imagine loving anyone else in this entire world."

"I love you too," Pylades responded. "But for me it is not the same, you know."

"I know," replied Orestes. "Someday, perhaps soon, you will be king and marry, or marry and be king."

"But I will always love you."

"I know," said Orestes, *but not as much as I love you.*

Pylades kissed him, like a man with a young maiden, on his eyes, forehead, and lips—again and again. His hands caressed Orestes' back, rubbed his neck. They moaned as one, gasped as one, and sighed as one. Then they held each other with tenderness and love, as if this was how they would remain until the end of time and of the world. Orestes fell into the life-giving sleep of the dead.

#

When he awoke, it was with a dull ache in his head. "No sword fighting today," he moaned. "In fact, I would not mind giving that up altogether."

"You cannot let your father's sword gather dust or rust!" Pylades said, "Elektra won't let you."

"You're right, though I can't let her boss me around. But today and most days, I will spend time at the bow and arrow; I am stronger than she, and I shall practice just as hard. I shall excel at double the distance!"

"It is good to have goals, and you are already very good," his cousin rejoined with good humor. "But to hit the bull's eye a hundred times in a row at seventy paces is not reasonable,"

"Well, maybe fifty paces then."

Elektra joined them on the way to the archery range. The archers could move the targets from one end to the other so they would not have to shoot into the sun. But the sun was now high in the sky, so it did not matter for that autumn day. Orestes explained his new determination to shoot at fifty paces. He hit his target with every arrow, but none landed in the eye in the middle. Seeing the set of his jaw, however, Elektra and Pylades nodded to each other.

"How are your headaches and dreams?" she asked.

"One dream a week for two months and three this week. Someone is sending me a message," Orestes replied.

"We should go visit Father's grave," said his sister. "Don't you feel guilty that we have not done so all this time?"

"Why? Do you think he will speak from the underground to give us guidance?" Orestes' cynicism about traditional beliefs often disturbed Elektra, but she only said,

"At least we should pay our respects and pour libations, as is customary for the dead to receive. It is long overdue."

"Yes, but first, perhaps a visit to the temple in Delphi," said Orestes, offering an olive branch to what he knew were his sister's beliefs.

"It is only a small community temple," said Elektra.

"Our scouts report that this is where Apollo's seers come to develop their powers," interjected Pylades. "We should consult them. Perhaps while we are there, Apollo will grant Orestes a clearer vision."

"When should we go?" asked Elektra.

"How does the winter solstice sound? Wouldn't that be an auspicious time?" Pylades asked. "Or perhaps we should wait for warmer weather?"

"It depends on how much worse these headaches and nightmares become," said Orestes.

"What do we hope achieve?" asked his sister.

"I need to be sure that the god wants Clytemnestra dead. It would be a shame to assassinate the wrong person since everyone says it was Aigisthos who killed Agamemnon. Vengeance should fall on him, even though as Thyestes' son he had the right to kill the king." Orestes wrung his hands and turned around. "If Apollo wants the queen killed, I must know why. She is my mother, and killing her is the most sacrilegious thing a man can do."

*Orestes does not make such long speeches*, Elektra thought. *He and Pylades have talked over this matter many times.*

"Further," added Pylades, "if Apollo wants you to do anything, he should understand that you won't be able to do it with the hammers going in your head. Perhaps he could kill the queen himself."

"Hush, you do not want to get these headaches yourself," warned Elektra. "Do not provoke the gods! Let's go after the solstice if the rains are not too heavy."

#

Strophios listened to Orestes explain his dilemma as Pylades looked on. When his nephew finished, the king said, "I don't understand why the god would want you to kill your mother. One would think he intends vengeance on Aigisthos."

The king shook his head and ran his fingers through his hair. It had thinned but was still bushy behind his ears. He continued, "But you must know I will not ride with you on that adventure. Pylades may ride with you only to keep you company. I forbid him to raise his hand against either the king or the queen of Mycenae."

"What do you advise, Uncle, on the whole undertaking?"

"If you need clarity about who you have to kill, consult the oracle. Delphi is only two or three days away on horseback. But if you want help with any killing in Mycenae, you might consult your Uncle Menelaos, now that he has returned. He was much closer to your father than anyone ever was." Strophios tugged at his hair as if to massage his scalp.

"I want it clear Pylades should have no part in any fighting or killing. He will soon be king here in Phocis and cannot afford to make enemies in Mycenae even before he is king."

"Does it matter whether I go to Delphi first?"

"Orestes, pardon my bluntness, but you are thinking of killing either the king or the queen of Mycenae, possibly both. You are then going to become the king yourself. You need to learn that being king involves hard decisions, because you must make them by yourself. Whether you go to Delphi or to Sparta—or sleep on your left or right side—these are the easy ones!"

"Come, Orestes, we can decide on the way," intervened Pylades as his lover blushed at the rebuke. "My father speaks the truth, and you would have come to the same conclusion soon. Do not let Apollo's temper unnerve you!"

This smooth change to the flow of the conversation pleased the king. Having celebrated his sixtieth summer, he now counted on Pylades to assume a more active role in ruling Phocis. However much the princes loved each other, things would change soon.

Orestes had now spent sixteen winters, more than half his life, in the idyllic hills of adolescence in Phocis and would have to descend to the uncertain plains of adulthood in Mycenae. Pylades and Elektra busied themselves with quick errands to the kitchen while waiting for him to come out of the fog of his thoughts.

"My father will send one of his commanders to keep us company," reported Pylades as they left the king to prepare for their journey.

"I think that would be helpful, even though with our bows and arrows, not to mention swords and shields, we can fend for ourselves," Elektra remarked. "I'll gather up extra cloaks and blankets to bring along."

"I shall see if the kitchen maids can arrange some packages of food for us," Pylades announced as he walked away towards the domestic quarters of the palace.

The commander sent to accompany them had an aunt, his father's youngest sister, married to a retired guardsman in the colony in Delphi. They had moved there when the king asked them to join the community to gather information and send information to Phocis. The commander had visited often and knew the way very well. He also had a younger sister in Mycenae married to a member of the palace guard.

# 11: DELPHI

Three small birds flew away as the party departed. With the king's blessings, Pylades, Orestes, Elektra, and the commander rode to Delphi. It was only a two-day ride from the palace, but they might have to wait for the seers, or perhaps for the god himself, to appear.

On the second day, they reached a break in the woods on a slope in the foothills of the Parnassus range over which the sun rose to shine on Phocis. In the brilliance of the midday sun, they saw a large natural hollow. This appeared as if the gods had scalloped it from the slope to prepare for large congregations, or gatherings for speech, drama, or music. Olive trees and oaks gave way to birches and pines. "There is nothing more inspiring than that small group of birch trees in the fall," said the commander. "They are not common around Phocis, but by some fancy of the gods or chance of the weather, these here are as majestic as those in the north of Thessaly."

"Thank you, Commander," replied Pylades in a kind but firm voice. "Perhaps we shall return to see them this fall or the next, but now we must move on."

"I feel something eerie and yet inviting," Orestes announced, "almost as if the ground will open up and we will find ourselves in a very special place. Do you not feel it?" Pylades and the commander shook their heads, but Elektra cocked her head and closed her eyes.

"This place feels as if it is very full of secrets that could be, might be, revealed," she said, as if distracted. "Perhaps we are to meet someone or something special."

A small cluster of huts among the trees below the natural amphitheater housed those who had gathered to devote themselves to the worship of Apollo. Many of them did not aspire to become seers but would serve those who did. They all herded sheep, gathered corn and herbs, cut wood for fire and shelter, and performed the many chores that kept the community alive and comfortable. Across the hill, another smaller community had gathered, worshippers of Dionysius who maintained a respectful distance. This was Delphi.

Upon their arrival at the huts, Kalkhas surprised them, emerging from one hut and greeting the travelers. It was as if he had been waiting for them, and he invited the three royal youths to stay with him in the largest building. This served as a gathering hall for the community but had small rooms for guests. He nodded to acknowledge the commander, who trotted off to another hut.

He said to Orestes and Elektra, "It has been a long time, over seventeen summers I reckon, since the armada sailed for Troy and I last saw you. You were children then. How old are you now, Orestes?"

"Twenty-eight, come the summer solstice," replied Orestes. "Elektra will be twenty-three." He then introduced Pylades, and Kalkhas showed them around the group of huts. After getting their bearings and making the acquaintance of several of the villagers, they made themselves comfortable for the evening in the gathering hall.

"Prepare to sleep well. Lord Apollo is likely to visit. If he does, you must not respond and, this is most important, do not question or resist his command. I will talk with you all tomorrow. You can ask me all your questions then," announced Kalkhas as he bade them goodnight.

A strong magical, spiritual sense enveloped the slope. Orestes had sensed this on the way; now everyone felt it. The colors seemed sharper and deeper, the water appeared wetter, if that was possible, and the silences appeared pregnant with the promise of revelations to come. After dark, one could almost hear a hum of everything ready to speak.

[*Apollo*]
Forget what you think you know about the gods.
Mortal men need to know only that they must obey.
All-Powerful Zeus who ordains, must guide your ways.
Time was, you were unfinished and unruly,
Your laws were still not in tune with the Divine.
The earth was young, and men and gods mingled often.
Chronos, Uranos, and Zeus; their stories filled your past.
Many ages have passed, it is time for fresh stories.
As the gods consort less than before with men,
So new laws must frame your life, your loves, and your death.
For you, Orestes, one thing is clear and inescapable—
You must avenge your father and your king, not sparing
Even your mother. Do not let pity deter you
Or the old tales distract, those told
At your nurse's knees or around campfires—
Tales of what your heroes and gods of old did or
Suffered or feared. Only one task matters.
Avenge your father and king; kill that woman, faithless
To her husband, her lord and master by laws and oaths
Most binding. Failure will mean agony unimaginable.
You have received many warnings, now act.
Beware! Beware! Beware! Beware! Catastrophe!

Orestes started and looked to his companions. No one else appeared to have heard or felt this communication. Was it only his dream? Pylades smiled at him while Elektra gazed all around.

He said, "But when will it end? Aigisthos was avenging his father and brothers, was he not?" Orestes blurted out, forgetting Kalkhas' caution that he was not to interrupt, to question.

"Do not speak, Orestes," cried out Elektra, too late.

A throb of pain that exploded into the most blinding and nauseating that Orestes had ever felt in his nightmares bloomed in his head. Every tooth in his mouth screamed to fall out; his eardrums shrieked with pain; his skull felt as if it would explode from his neck. Though he did not dream again that night, he remained awake and conscious of that throbbing, blinding, nauseating agony.

Everything Elektra or Pylades said, every small sound they made, bounced in his skull. He wanted Pylades to hold him, he wanted no one to touch him. He wanted to tear himself from limb to limb, but he could not move. He would, if he could, dash his head against the floor or the pillars that held up the walls and roof-beams, but neither his arms nor his feet would obey his will. The sulfurous torture in his head consumed his will.

Pylades looked everywhere for Kalkhas but did not find him until daybreak. The seer looked like death itself; white-faced, covered in sweat, his eyes hollow. But he walked with grim determination toward the meeting hall. In his hands, he carried a flask of honey and a small vial of black paste.

"This is a gift of Morpheus, obtained at great price from far away," the seer said. "I have little of it." He knelt by Orestes and poured some honey into a cupped hand, into which he mixed a fingernail of the black paste. He fed this to Orestes, saying, "You must do everything to keep this in your mouth until it melts down your throat. This paste will help with the pain. It may even help you sleep."

"How long will he be so?" asked Pylades in anguish and hopelessness.

"Five days."

"Do you have enough of that paste?"

"No."

Elektra got up and walked through the village, talking to the old women who were up. What did they use for the worst pains they ever felt? All the women agreed they could not imagine what Orestes was going through, that they did not know of such visions. But for a difficult childbirth, there was a common remedy. It was the only remedy even if it did not always work to satisfaction—the bark and leaves of the willow. Many of those of child-bearing age had a supply and contributed leaves, bark, and lore.

Thus, after the fourth day, when the seer's supply of black paste gave out, they started using the willow leaves and bark. These were not as strong as the gift of Morpheus, and so Orestes wailed and sobbed then more than ever. They also boiled mint and rosemary in the room where Orestes lay. These were old folk remedies to bring refreshment and perhaps relief from pain. Pylades had found some willow branches and cut pieces of these and placed them between Orestes' teeth so he would not bite his tongue. He watched his lover night and noon for those five days.

"What do we do now?" Pylades asked Kalkhas on the sixth day.

"I must make sure that Orestes understands what he has to do; then he must do it."

"And what is it he must do?"

"He must kill Clytemnestra."

Pylades had expected this but blurted out, "Seven years ago, Aigisthos said he killed Agamemnon. Shouldn't we take vengeance on him?"

Kalkhas looked into Pylades' eyes and said, "I have learned NEVER to question Lord Apollo. I imagine the same is true with any of the other gods. If you wish to seek a vision from

Agamemnon at his tomb, do so. But Orestes must kill Clytemnestra soon, or his nightmares will return. I can do nothing more for him, I will not even try."

"Killing his mother," objected Pylades with anxious concern, "will bring great pollution on his spirit. Will Apollo grant him absolution?"

"Of course, Lord Apollo will purify him. If, as old wives' tales have suggested, the Furies dare to harass Orestes, he is welcome to come here for sanctuary. Only here, you understand. This is Apollo's shrine now." Kalkhas declared this with finality.

"Where else would he go?" asked Pylades, seeking a second string for his bow.

"He might think of seeking shelter with the followers of Dionysius, whom some call *eleutherios*, the Liberator. You should know that is not a good idea."

"How," persisted Pylades, "do we ensure Agamemnon will grant us a vision?"

Kalkhas shrugged. "Men can make certain nothing about the gods or the dead. You should make a sacrifice first to Hermes, the messenger of the gods. He travels from Olympus to Hades as easily as anyone, and if he is willing, he could get Agamemnon to appear. I recommend this if you must consult Agamemnon's ghost, but I urge you to lose no more time."

"One last thing," asked Elektra. "We wish to seek help from our Uncle Menelaos."

"Yes, I too have heard he has reached Sparta at last, but he will give you little help," said the seer. "If it makes you feel better, Sparta is just two days past Mycenae. As long as you do not stop anywhere too long, Lord Apollo will not add to your burdens."

As Orestes seemed stronger the next day, Pylades and Elektra spoke with him about his mission as defined by Apollo and clarified by Kalkhas.

"I could not learn why he wants me to kill my mother," Orestes complained. "It is wrong and an impious deed."

"I don't think you should argue with a god, Orestes," observed Elektra. "Especially not with one who can inflict such pain on you."

"We should go to King Agamemnon's shrine as Kalkhas suggests and ask who killed the king." Pylades words carried the flat tone of defeat when a fighter realizes that there are no more choices.

"Yes, but first we have a hard ride to Sparta," concluded Elektra. "I wonder if Uncle Menelaos remembers us."

The sun shone brilliantly, and the birds sang lustily among the trees, which were all putting out their spring shoots. The storm clouds gathered and burst, refreshing life in Delphi. If the young royals had felt any foreboding when they entered the area, they now rode away with the sense that the world of trees and shrubs moved beyond the worries and anxieties that still clawed at their hearts.

# 12: SPARTA

The young royals rode hard for three days, skirting the mountains of Arcadia and passing by the Argolid region into the Laconian plain before they reached Sparta. They passed small farms in which peasants planted barley, and cabbage, garlic, and beans. Farmers prepared olive trees and grapevines for their summer growth and fruit-bearing. Every once in a while, a group of tall, dark green cypresses appeared, standing out against the other vegetation in the landscape still lush from the spring rainstorms. In a few weeks, the heat of summer would dry out the valleys and plains.

In Sparta, the party saw no walls. The traditions of the city demanded each man to be ready with sword, spear, and shield to defend his home. These were sturdy and simple; the smallest with four square rooms, five paces a side, and the largest with ten such rooms. The palace was about as large as ten of the largest houses. It lay a short ride, less time than a horse would take to drink after a hard morning or afternoon ride, beyond the southern edge of the city, amid a small cluster of huts.

Back from Troy six summers after Agamemnon, Menelaos and Helen welcomed Orestes and Elektra. A shy little girl, Hermione, appeared and her adoring parents presented her to them as their cousin. She had just celebrated her fifth winter and resembled her mother with her blonde curls and pink dimpled cheeks. Helen herself seemed to have aged very little.

Elektra thought, *perhaps the legend that Zeus was her real father is true.* Her aunt Helen held her and Orestes close for a long time and wept with them.

When Orestes spoke with Menelaos about avenging his father, however, the king of Sparta demurred. He had lost much of his hair and gained a few pounds, but remained the trim warrior of medium height that Orestes remembered. As the king of Sparta back from that war, he exerted himself daily, riding with his guards to the outlying farms. He was solicitous of the welfare of his people and troubled by rumors and signs that they blamed Helen for the war and all its woes.

Many a widow and fatherless family resented the woman they considered the source of their sorrow. Only the efforts of the king and the moral authority of old King Tyndareos kept them from showing their grievances. Helen's father, though ancient, kept the poise and carriage of one who strode with Hercules on a hoary tale of a mission together. Some elders of Sparta claimed to remember that time.

Menelaos frowned and shook his head, incredulous at Orestes' mission from Apollo.

"You cannot be serious!" cried the king of Sparta. "She is my sister-in-law. I can have nothing to do with your mission. You should also remember that though Tyndareos gave up his throne so I could be king, and is now ancient, he is still very much alive. He loves both his daughters and may very well demand that I march out against you! I cannot ride with you on this and will not lift a finger to help this expedition of yours."

Orestes pleaded that this was the burden that Apollo had laid on him, that when he had questioned it, the god had been terrible in punishing him. Menelaos rubbed his face and pulled his hair, uncomprehending. "How can that be? Everyone tells me it was Aigisthos who killed my brother!"

"I have tried once to argue with a god," replied Orestes. "I have no desire to try again, although the thought of killing my mother appalls and terrifies me."

"Perhaps we could offer a sacrifice of a hundred bulls to Apollo," suggested Menelaos. "I am more than willing to help you with that."

"Kalkhas did not suggest that there was any room to bargain with Apollo," replied Orestes as he rolled his head to loosen the muscles of his neck.

"That old seer? The same man who advised Agamemnon to sacrifice Iphigenia." There was bitterness in Menelaos' voice, for he had adored his niece. He had not blamed his beloved brother, however, and placed all his anger on the seer. "Well, I will not involve myself in how you deal with the gods or their seers. But please do not mention this to Helen. The Spartans, like all the Greeks, are sullen every time she celebrates a public festival. Her sister has been her only champion outside this palace." Then with wonder and bemusement the king added, "Aigisthos has accompanied Clytemnestra on her visits and behaved with great courtesy."

"We will go to our father's grave to see if he will speak to us and help us understand why Apollo has determined that I must kill the queen," Orestes said, with his head down. "I do not want to do that at all, but Apollo is implacable."

Menelaos thought for a while and observed, "The will of the gods is a dark mystery. You should summon Hermes first, for only he can travel between the living and the dead. You will need to offer a sacrifice."

"We are prepared to do that," said Orestes.

Menelaos nodded, "Let me see if we can find some myrrh or similar incense to add to your sacrifice to entice Hermes. That is all I can or will do to help you." Sparta, unlike cosmopolitan Mycenae and its inhabitants, had little need for goods from afar. They clung to the poor soil around their small city, perhaps in the belief that it developed their character. Of course, they distrusted traders.

Eventually, the palace maids found a small box of myrrh and frankincense worth a princely sum of silver and gold. It lay in the jumble in a storeroom of the palace filled with things Menelaos had not finished unpacking from his expedition to Troy.

"Take it," urged Menelaos, "I cannot do more to help you."

That night, the king and queen of Sparta entertained the party from Phocis, fed them and gave them their choice of rooms in the palace. Menelaos asked to see their bows and arrows.

"We did not have many of these at the war. Most of us had no use for them. Ulysses said he left a magnificent bow in Ithaca that only he could string," the king shrugged. "But this was how Paris killed Achilles and avenged Hector." With a little reluctance, he allowed himself to be coaxed into recounting that story and would have continued except that he noticed Helen's growing uneasiness. Stories of Troy stirred up difficult memories for her.

"Your bows will win you great honor, I trust," Menelaos remarked, changing the subject from that great war. "They look well made to me, though I know very little about them. How did you come upon them?"

"Twelve winters ago, we heard about these things from a trader and wanted to make them to play with," explained Pylades. "One of the palace servants was from north of Thessaly and was familiar with them. He made us some for play but insisted we should have 'real bows' if we would allow him to search for the right wood. My father sent him with a guard while he searched for yew or ash trees with the right length of straight trunks or branches."

"Those trees grow all over," laughed Menelaos.

"Yes, but he was very particular about how old and straight the trees had to be," continued Pylades. "He returned in a few weeks with enough to make ten bows. We practiced with them over the years. Elektra and Orestes are much better at hitting their targets than I."

"I'm sure Ulysses, wherever he is, would approve," the Spartan king responded with a slight catch in his voice as his fellow warrior's long disappearance troubled him. "Now, perhaps you would all like to retire. There are days of hard riding ahead of you." The queen kissed them each tenderly as they left.

"She is so beautiful—so radiant and affectionate," exclaimed Pylades. "I can see why Paris and the Trojans fought to keep her."

"Even though adultery is a serious crime, more so than the breach of hospitality," added Orestes grimly.

"We hear that a lot," reflected Pylades, "but it does not seem right. The blame is usually applied to the woman even though there are always two parties involved."

"I remember her hair being thicker and her face completely unlined," Elektra chimed in, and then looking flustered, said. "But I was just a child then, what would I know?"

The young men looked at her and smiled knowingly to each other as she blushed a deep red.

"Well, it's time for bed."

That night, Orestes dreamed yet again of breasts and vipers, but though he woke up shaking and sweating, there was no pounding headache.

"A nudge from Apollo?" asked Pylades as they comforted each other.

Orestes nodded and said with a shaky voice, "A rather gentle one this time."

"It is a good thing we are at last going to Mycenae," said Pylades.

Two days later, the three royals and their companion arrived at Mycenae, to Agamemnon's shrine in an olive grove near the city. When at last they approached it, the commander suggested they camp and wait by the olive trees while he called on his sister. He wished also to find out what they might face when they approached the palace. He returned early the next day. To the alarm of the young royals, a Mycenaean soldier accompanied him.

"It's the herald," cried out Orestes. "He came with the night watchman and others when we were just starting with our archery lessons."

"He is now a senior member of the palace guard in Mycenae," the commander reassured them as he sensed their fear. "But do not be alarmed, I have not betrayed you. This is my sister's husband, and he will not hinder you."

Agathon smiled warmly at them and explained, "I do not understand my lord Aigisthos. He knows you are here and sends me to protect you. As a sworn member of the palace guards, I will not raise my sword against him. But he has ordered me to give you all the assistance and protection possible."

"He knows why we are here?" asked Orestes, his voice shaking.

Agathon nodded. "He has been expecting you. Sharp eyes sighted your approach yesterday. He says to remind you he and the queen are ready to leave—"

"But the gods have ordered me to kill the queen."

Agathon blanched when he heard this, but repeated to them his own orders. "Nevertheless, Aigisthos has ordered me to be your guide and to protect you from any overzealous guards. Of that, you need not fear, for he also ordered everyone in the palace not to raise a sword against you."

"I can scarcely believe that," declared Orestes. Pylades nodded and voiced his own skepticism.

"How can we trust this king? What is his true aim?"

"He says he wishes to end the cycle of killing and vengeance," responded Agathon. "He and the queen are ready to leave the palace. Such an act is unheard of. I too find it difficult to believe."

"We must seek counsel from our father," cried Elektra. The others looked at her and each other and nodded.

"Have you eaten?" asked Agathon.

The commander from Phocis now hurried to unpack a sack filled with freshly baked bread, cheese, dried figs, and olives. He also had two skins filled with the local wine mixed with water. As he distributed these, he announced, "From my sister."

"There is no need to rush unless you fear Apollo's impatience," remarked Agathon with half a smile. "My wife's brother, the commander, has told me about your sufferings in Delphi. The god seems to have taken matters into his own hands. I have brought what you may need to seek Hermes' help, though I do not think he will thwart Apollo. I am told by those who know that although they are both sons of Zeus, Apollo is older and stronger."

"Do those things still matter?" asked Orestes.

As Agathon shrugged, Pylades complained in as mild a tone as he could find, "I would think the gods might have given up their petty rivalries and their schemes on behalf of their favorites among humans. Look at what these emotions and motives produced in Troy."

"We should not be so eager to judge the gods," muttered the commander sent by Strophios. "It is not safe."

# 13: THE LIBATION BEARERS

It was late afternoon by the time the young royals and their two trusty companions approached the olive grove where Agamemnon's memorial stood. They were all dressed in white chitons; Agathon and the commander had their swords tucked in the folds of their loose tunics. The greatest heat of the late spring day had passed, so a pleasant coolness mingled with the scent of laurel refreshed the solemn group. They stopped and made themselves inconspicuous as they heard women chanting. Soon, a small group of twenty women, dressed in black, came into view.

[*All the Mourners*]
We hail and laud thee, O Agamemnon, king of men.
You, who returned victorious from your mighty labors
On the broad plains of Troy, as you did from
Your many expeditions to establish
The will of Zeus throughout this land.
O king, we have maintained your shrine,
As enjoined by Lord Aigisthos and his Lady Clytemnestra.
At every new moon, we have come
To honor your memory with fresh libations,
To sweeten the air with fresh boughs of laurel,
And to sweep away grime and filth, from man or beast,
Or from the wind and the weather, that should foul your memorial
Or tarnish your memory.
We implore you to keep the city safe and the plains fertile!
We beseech you to guard over us against pestilence,
And swords and spears.
We pray peace be with your spirit, for you have

Made all who live in the Argolid proud.
Hail Agamemnon, king of men!


The women swept around the shrine and then poured their urns of wine as a libation to the late king. The Greek women separated from the Trojan captives to begin a fresh chorus.


*Ou-ai*, listen also to our woe for our grief overflows.
We, whose fathers, husbands, lovers, and brothers followed you;
We, who have waited in vain for their return.
Our number is great; those here are but the few
Who have sought the protection of the palace
From hunger and homelessness. No one can protect us
From the gnawing pain of sorrow and loss.
It is not greater than those of our number
Who enjoy the comfort of remaining family.
They suffer still from anguish of those they have lost.
But our eyes have grown dim from the tears we have shed—
Our voices hoarse from the cries we have raised.
Our hearts have dried up with our hopes and love.
Only these shells remain—bereft, benighted, and beyond hope.
Are our fathers, husbands, lovers and brothers with you?
Do they do you honor as we do? As we must, by command
Of our lord and our lady?
They followed you gladly for love of their king;
We beseech you to share with them the libations we have brought.


"That is not what they should chant," Agathon remarked, "though I will not fault them for the desolation in their hearts and prayers." Pylades, shocked at this rough lesson in statecraft, set his face grimly as Elektra's eyes moistened. Orestes stood stunned. The Trojan women now took up the chant.

*Ou-ai, ou-ai,* hear us, most fearful king of men.
You who led those myriad ships and men against us.
Foolish Paris gave you your moment, and you grasped it.
Hector and Priam loved him too dearly to abandon him.
To what end? *Ou-ai,* to what end?
Those we loved most greatly, our fathers, husbands, lovers and brothers—
All fell before your swords and flames.
They made you pay horribly, they did.
Us, you and your men gathered as trophies and war brides.
Half of us could not bear the thought of such fate.
They embraced us, then threw themselves
Into Poseidon's watery clutch.
Half of those left among us were sick and lost at sea,
Joining their captors in that briny sepulcher.
Yet another half of those who sailed
Have since succumbed to taunts, torment, and terror
As prisoners of war. We remain,
Who do not deserve better. We have seen how
Those who Troy captured before Priam's walls have fared.
We know the cruelties that their jailors visited on those who
Fell into its snares or yielded to its armies.
We who remain of your trophies and can still walk
Have joined in pouring the libations to you,
King of men, that we may join in their sorrow
And share in their grief. Know this, that the libations we poured,
We have poured for you and for ourselves.
*Ou-ai, ou-ai!*

The women regrouped, Greek and Trojan together despite being separated by race. Tragic fate bound them. Thus, they recessed from the grove. A somber silence fell upon the group, broken by Agathon.

"My lord Orestes, it will be dark in a while. If we are to seek the aid of Hermes and Agamemnon, we must start now." They brought the two lambs that had been drugged and kept in a sack out and cut them into six pieces each for the sacrifice to the god Hermes.

Strophios' commander organized the others in building a makeshift altar and prepared the fire for the sacrifice. Then he suggested, "Orestes, you and your sister should cut off a lock each of your hair and prepare these with wine and olive oil for your father's ghost. It has long been our custom."

So, these royal siblings prepared themselves. They had seen it done but never had it been their own need, nor had such need ever been so great.

The incense that their Uncle Menelaos provided was the ideal accompaniment to the sacrifice of the lamb. The smoke and air around them shimmered, and Hermes revealed himself addressing Orestes—

[*Hermes*]
Grandson of Atreus, your sacrifice pleases me;
And your intentions are clear and worthy.
You desire me to fetch your father; that is easy.
(Much easier by far than what Atreus asked for.
He badgered us in a way I think you will not.)
Your father's word, whether hard or easy, is less certain.
He will speak and may allay your fear and doubt.
He may say much or little to answer your question.
But you must be clear about this one condition—

You may not detain him long, however willing
He might be. His place is not here among the living.

Hermes faded from their eyes. The ghastly image of Agamemnon appeared, pale and bearing signs of his last wounds. The sharp slash across his neck that had cut the arteries of his neck and his windpipe and also the jagged edge of the wound to his right armpit.

"Father, we pray our offerings ease your—" Orestes began.

[*The ghost of Agamemnon*]
You seek to know why Lord Apollo demands
Your mother's death when all say it was
My cousin that slew me. Do not be confused.
Aigisthos cut my throat and caused my death
After we had battled most fiercely.
But he never would have succeeded, pardon
My boast, had not Clytemnestra thrust her broad dagger
Here to disable me. *Ou-ai, ou-ai!*
My cousin also says he and the queen
Will leave the throne to you. Beware
The command of Bright, All-seeing Apollo!
More I cannot say, but must leave.
I only regret that I brought
The lovely Cassandra into this
Tangled and murderous web. *Ou-ai, ou-ai!*

The ghost of the king raised his right arm to reveal again the fullness of the ugly wound inflicted by the queen. Then he faded from their view.

#

Late as it was, Aigisthos summoned Aristides and the captain of the guards to attend him when Agathon returned to the palace with his report.

The herald turned palace guard had left the young royals at their camp by Agamemnon's grove, in the care of Strophios' commander. He told them a half-truth, that he was returning to his wife and would be back to accompany them in the morning. They prepared for one last night of sleep before fulfilling the doom that Apollo had laid upon Orestes.

"The prince and his group should be easy to capture or kill," declared the captain of the guards. Four men sat in the silence that followed as the torches flickered in the corner of the great hall of the palace. Three intent faces turned to Aigisthos. His own, as usual, betrayed nothing as he gave thought to his next action or command.

"No," he said. "The Lord Apollo has taken this matter is out of our hands."

"It is the queen's life!" exclaimed Aristides with concern.

"I will not let her die alone," replied Aigisthos, his lips set.

"Are you going to let the young prince walk in and kill you both?" the captain asked in disbelief.

Aigisthos did not answer but turned to Agathon and asked, "What did you learn about the prince and his intentions?"

Agathon squirmed with his face screwed up, but Aigisthos had only a smile for him. The herald drew a deep breath for courage,

"He said he had visions from Apollo for several months. These suggest that the prince is himself the 'viper that bites the queen.' He had an episode during which he questioned Apollo that resulted in a week of torment. Elektra is adamant that he no longer has a choice. He has to kill the queen or die himself."

Aigisthos nodded thoughtfully and said, "The queen has had several dreams of a viper biting her."

"Why won't the gods leave us in peace?" Agathon blurted out, then paled, and looked down in confusion. He trembled.

"Why won't they?" asked Aigisthos, nodding sadly. "They goad us into war; stir desire for slaughter and conquest within our hearts..."

"My lord," Aristides interrupted. "Is it wise to accuse the gods of all our misfortunes?"

The king paused and reflected, "I think there is enough blame to share. We or our fathers have made bad decisions, and we must now suffer the consequences." He turned to ask Agathon, "Do you think the prince will pursue us if the queen and I leave Mycenae?"

"But—" said the captain of the guards.

"I do not wish to order you to stand in the way of a man with a mission from Far-seeing Apollo," Aigisthos said to the captain. The loyal man gaped.

"My lord," Agathon replied, "I believe the gods have marked Orestes and they will not rest. So, I venture to guess, neither can he."

The captain of the guards grunted in disbelief; counselor Aristides' face darkened as his frown grew deeper. The king reflected for several heartbeats.

"So be it," he declared at last. "The queen and her ladies have offered prayers to Zeus. If he answers them, Orestes cannot hurt us. If not, nothing can save us. I do not see that we can gain anything by running away from this meeting with Orestes."

The shadows deepened in the silence that followed, though the torches burned just as brightly. The king closed his eyes. His feelings shone clearer. Anguish over the final fate of the queen, doubt of his own resolve, fear for the inevitable consequences. He grimaced as he opened his mouth in a wordless cry, a silent howl. The three men brought into his confidence, watched and waited. In time, he achieved control over his doubts and feelings.

He opened his eyes and announced, "Agathon, now more than ever, the prince needs you. I release you from service in the palace guards and ask that you stay with him and do whatever you can to keep him from harm. He is of the House of Agamemnon and of Atreus, which you must help preserve. My oath to my father did not include him." He added with a wry smile, "I do not recommend challenging Apollo."

The king stood up and paced with a spring in his steps, "However the gods will it, the queen and I shall remain or Orestes will be king. I authorize Aristides to preside over the council of elders if I die before Orestes becomes king. May the gods guide him. I ask the captain of the guards to give them full support." He looked at them and waited for their acknowledgement. Then he dismissed them with equanimity and resolve.

"I expect to spend the next few hours with the queen."

# 14: AGAMEMNON AVENGED

"Good morning, my lord Aigisthos," said Clytemnestra with a grave smile as she approached the king seated at a table by a window.

"Good morning, beloved. I trust you slept well."

"I did, to my surprise," said the queen as she reached to run her fingers through Aigisthos' hair and bent to kiss him.

She pulled him to her breasts and hugged him, then sighed and moaned as he kissed her nipples through her chiton. He kissed his way to her face as he rose, and then they made their four-legged way to their bed.

#

The sun was high when the king and queen rose again. The queen asked, "What can you see through that window?"

"That it is a beautiful spring morning and promises to be a wonderful day."

"Nothing to fear?" asked the queen with a quiver in her voice.

"We decide what we will be afraid of, remember?"

"The gods have sent my son to kill us and we *decide* not to be afraid?"

"I believe that's what Hector did on the day he rode out to face Achilles. He may have said some extra prayers; no doubt Andromache did, as you and your ladies have done."

"I have no confidence that the gods have heard our prayers. Did you send the guards away?"

"Yes. If the gods have decided in our favor, we will not need them. If our fate is otherwise, they cannot protect us. So..."

The queen burst into tears and collapsed on Aigisthos' lap. "I love you so much. I cannot bear the thought of being separated from you."

"They will not separate us, unless death has the power to rip the bonds of love—my lady, my queen. While I draw breath, we will not be parted." A servant approached and announced a small party bearing only wooden sticks.

"Show them to the main hall," Aigisthos instructed the maid with weary courtesy. "I guess those 'wooden sticks' would be their bows and arrows that we heard about seven autumns ago." The queen restrained her sobs and managed a weak smile as she responded, "They should be proficient by now." They went hand in hand to the great hall of the palace to face the party from Phocis.

#

The young royals and their companions arose with the sun that fateful morning. They had a breakfast of bread, cheese, and wine, though no one was hungry. Orestes' mood swung between anxiety to complete his task and dread of what he had to do. Elektra trembled, anxious for Orestes to fulfill Apollo's task. Agathon looked pained and strained. His brother-in-law, the commander sent by Strophios, and Pylades were the only ones with clear feelings about the task ahead. They packed and rode in silence into the city.

Leaving the Phocian commander with the horses, the others walked toward the palace. The old stones that made up the walls impressed the young royals.

"I've seen nothing like this," marveled Pylades. "Your Uncle Menelaos lives in a large house, but it is smaller even than our palace in Phocis. This is huge. They must have hewn these rocks and those of the city walls from the same quarries. These walls look like they have resisted much and will last forever."

"I had forgotten what an imposing building this is," agreed Elektra. "It looks as if it would stand a very long time." They decided that Pylades and Agathon would remain just outside the palace with all their swords, including the one Agamemnon had swung at Troy.

Orestes and Elektra entered through the main doorway; the prince with a bow and arrow, while his sister carried a spare bow and a quiver of arrows.

"Welcome," cried out the king. His voice rang in that space that served as the main audience hall and could hold over a hundred seats at large banquet tables. It was empty, except for the imposing wooden throne at the end furthest from the main entrance. The king and queen had entered through a side entrance. This was where Aigisthos and Agamemnon had fought their epic battle, slashing and thrusting, dodging sometimes around the sturdy columns.

"Thank you," replied Orestes, his face drawn and his hair disheveled.

"Where is your friend Pylades?"

"He decided he should remain outside as this is a family matter," declared Orestes, who trembled like a goat brought to a sacrifice. He looked around and asked, "Is this where my father died?"

"Are you certain that you want to proceed, Orestes?" asked his mother. "You know I cannot let you kill Aigisthos without making you kill me first."

"Apollo's bidding was that I should kill you," he replied with a confidence he did not feel. He shook his head as if to expel from his mind ugly thoughts like a horse trying to shake off flies.

"Your own mother, Orestes?" queried Clytemnestra, with more surprise than fear. "One who gave you life, and at whose breasts you fed before you could eat anything else? Do you not know what a heinous crime that is?"

"You shamed me with your adultery!" Orestes shouted, his voice shaking with confusion and panic.

"Don't be silly, Orestes! What do you call your father's actions with Cassandra and those before her—the camp followers and trophies of war?" shouted his mother in reply. "You men think society can find only women guilty of adultery!"

"I have no choice," mumbled her son, sobbing. "Apollo has warned me of the consequences of disobedience. He said the gods want to improve the morals of men."

"By taking away from us choice in how we conduct ourselves or in what we do?" muttered Aigisthos in a low voice. "The gods are more insane than I thought." Then he spoke up, "Don't mind me. You must do what Apollo has commanded you to do. I am king now, but I remember well when I was a soldier. I understand orders and all that. But I will not let you kill your mother... Kill me first!"

"Aigisthos, no," cried the queen as Orestes found the resolve to string his bow and brought it up with an arrow nocked. In a fluid motion, the king swung Clytemnestra behind him so he faced Orestes. It was forty paces between the two men. The arrow, aimed at the king's heart, was a little low and pierced his abdomen. Dark red, almost black stains spread from the wound through his chiton.

"Kill me too," shrieked the queen.

Moving like one whose will was no longer his own, Orestes raised his bow a second time and shot. This time, the arrow found its mark in the queen's chest and she fell as bright red blood stained her tunic.

The stricken couple scratched along the floor and crawled into each other's arms.

"I love you, Aigisthos," choked the queen as she struggled to find breath. "You make my toes smile."

"More; I wanted to love you more," wept Aigisthos, fighting to remain conscious. He pulled the queen closer and laid his head on her shoulder as he slipped out of consciousness, out of life.

The earth trembled as if to mark the passing of the queen and her lover. The air outside shimmered and appeared to Pylades to thin out, as if a barrier that guarded the world as he knew it was dissolving. He ran with their two other companions into the palace and shouted, "Orestes, we must leave. Something unholy is happening."

The prince had slumped down to sit on the floor and gazed up, looking lost. He had so bent his will toward the task Apollo had assigned him, he had no inkling of what he would do next. "What?"

"Monsters," said Pylades, "appearing from out of the earth."

"The Furies," whispered the commander. "No one has seen them within memory, but I remember old stories about them. They arrive to torment and punish evil doers."

"Why, who, what?" spluttered the uncomprehending prince.

"They are coming to the palace," cried Agathon. "Old folks warned about them, and the retribution they bring to those who commit horrible crimes. Now would be a good time for Apollo to show up."

"Are they real?" asked Elektra. "I mean, can they harm Orestes? I thought they only existed in our heads."

"As Apollo only exists in our heads," protested Orestes, whining in frustration and despair.

"We must leave at once," urged Agathon.

"Can we outrun them?" worried Orestes aloud.

"It is better than just standing here," declared Pylades.

"Where should we go?" Orestes asked.

"Kalkhas said Apollo would purify and protect Orestes," exclaimed Elektra. "Let's go to Delphi."

"Agamemnon's grave and Hercules' grove are on the way," reasoned Agathon. "We might get some help at those places along the way."

As the party approached the grave of the late king, a voice they could all hear in their minds greeted them.

[*Hermes*]
My brother Apollo is careless and hasty;
He leaves me to attend to what he has left
Undone. To purify you, however, is beyond
My scope. But I can speed you on your way and hinder
Those ancients who hasten to suck you dry of your
Life and soul. Gruesome they appear, awesome their power,
Though they have been long out of human sight and mind.
I remember them well but cannot say whether
Even Apollo can prevail against the Erinyes.
Do not think less of the Olympian gods,
If we confess to our limitations. Farewell.

"Did you all hear that?" cried the Phocian commander. "The gods be praised!" Their horses snorted with new vigor, and they themselves felt renewed, young again. They felt their senses newly alert, urgent and unquenchable, as with the passion of first love. On the Furies, Hermes cast a spell that made them drowsy and sluggish, feeling each season of their long and baleful existence as a decade, each decade as a century. The young royals sped on to Hercules' grove and beyond, riding into the night.

"What's so special about that grove?" wondered Agathon out loud, hoping for an answer from the older man. But it was Pylades who remembered a lesson from a tutor to the royal youths.

"After Hercules fulfilled the twelve tasks required of him as purification from ritual pollution, the stories say, he came come to those white poplars. Their leaves are only white on one side, they are green on the other. He made himself a crown of those leaves."

"What twelve tasks?" panted Agathon.

"I'll tell you when we have more leisure," replied Pylades after catching a quick breath.

"What ritual pollution?" persisted Agathon.

"He killed his wife and daughters," stated Pylades in a burst.

"Hercules?" gasped Agathon. "Our greatest hero?"

Pylades only nodded.

"He fought monsters and evil beasts!"

Again Pylades nodded, saving his breath as they cantered up a steep slope.

"Sounds like another long story," muttered Agathon as Pylades, again, only nodded. The party found reserves of strength unknown to them. With only brief rest stops, the riders continued through the next days and nights until they reached Delphi.

When they arrived, Pylades briefed Kalkhas, who led them into the shrine the worshippers of Apollo had built. He made them comfortable and bade them rest while he communed with the god.

# 15: THE FURIES DEFY APOLLO

Orestes and his companions awoke to a noisy commotion in the shrine. They saw Kalkhas and his assistants confronting creatures that looked like old women dressed in many layers of rags and covered with snakes. Perhaps it was so because when they spoke everyone heard hisses that almost drowned out their voices. Their appearance suggested they should smell of sulphur and hell-fire, yet around them swirled a smell of the earth, of deep and old earth.

"You have no right to be here," Kalkhas intoned. "We dedicated this shrine to Lord Apollo, god of the golden light and son of Zeus Almighty. Bright Apollo himself has purified Orestes, whom you seek for your foul purposes. You have no power over him!"

[*The Furies*]
What would you know about our powers?
You are but Apollo's lackey.
We are more ancient even than Zeus,
Though we bow before his thunderbolts.
Him we seek has killed his own
Mother. Such pollution Apollo—
Even though he rides with the sun
And spreads great pestilence among
The armies and cities of men—
Cannot forgive, cleanse or absolve.
One who has murdered his mother
Is damned forever. We own
His soul and life. Of old we were
And are devourers of such monsters.

The appearance of Apollo himself, radiant in anger and self-importance, interrupted the Furies, those ancient divine beings that tended to the fate of men and the world. Bright Apollo said,

[*Apollo*]
Do such crones as you dare intrude into my shrine?
You do not recognize the passing of power to
A new era. Even as Chronos has supplanted
Ouranos, and Zeus, father of us all, vanquished him.
You presume to belittle my power to absolve what you call
Pollution. Know then that Zeus has judged
Men to lack order and reverence for life and for
The gods. The senseless cycles of murder must end.
Such vengeance as you speak of is too little
Or too much and hinge on inflamed passions.

His audience, however, was far from cowed by his appearance or his claims and retorted,

[*The Furies*]

We hear what you have to say
And long have we observed
That what you do
Mock your own lofty goals.
Zeus himself has favored Hercules,
And waged war on Priam's city.
Why else do you favor Agamemnon?
And now you wish to exempt his son
From full and just retribution
For slaying his own mother. Pah!
How just and proper is that!

[*Apollo*]

Agamemnon was far from being my favorite among
The Greeks. He prolonged the agony of war before
Priam's gate by refusing the ransom offered by Chryses
My priest, who pleased me with his manifold devotion,
For his daughter, Chryseis. The fool claimed she was more
Fit to be his queen than Clytemnestra. So he
Boasted and kept Chryseis to feed his lust for a year
Despite the pestilence I sent among the Greeks.
Then when his chiefs and men persuaded him to
Accept her father's ransom, he took Briseis from
Brilliant Achilles—Agamemnon, that fool, that idiot.
He was effective as leader and king, but rudderless
As a man. I do this not for him, but
To uphold all fathers, kings, and Zeus.

[*The Furies*]

Then why protect his son Orestes?
For the son killed his mother.
Are mothers less than fathers and kings?
Do men not avenge their mothers?

[*Apollo*]

Because she began the slaughter of her own lord,
Agamemnon. Orestes' sin is less,
He had to avenge his father and king.

[*The Furies*]

The queen's stain is not the same as her son's.
Man and wife are not kin. Though wrong

This sin is less than matricide.
Our role is to avenge the slaughter
Of those who should be cherished—
The worst of crimes, the most impious.

[*Apollo*]

Do you then belittle the bonds of marriage?
The gods made such sacred—Aphrodite, Hera,
Zeus himself, even Hestia, Zeus' older sister?
Further, to the sacred rituals between man and wife
Consider the vows of parents, of clans and nations—
These are what bind man and wife, not their kinship.
Your fine distinction is weak; to take
Any life is murder. But to kill a
King who must, Zeus-like, give order to a city,
We deem, is a crime that demands vengeance. Father Zeus
and
I urged Orestes on to his glorious deed.

[*The Furies*]

You call glorious what we assert
To be heinous murder. A mother
Is closer and dearer than anyone
And ought to receive reverence above all.

[*Apollo*]

Not so, for a child is born of the seed of a man,
Who places that seed in a woman only temporarily
Until it is ready for the world and its fate.
The mother gives nothing but a space for the seed

Which she gives up when time is ripe and birth fitting.

[*The Furies*]

Your words are childish and ignorant—
Laughable if they were not so vile.

[*Apollo*]

Athena, goddess of wisdom, was not born of a mother.

[*The Furies*]

The exception that proves the rule.
But we will stay and bandy words
No more with you. You cannot cleanse
Orestes from the pollution of the
Murder of his mother. Surrender
Him to us—we will suck out his
Stained gore, polluted as it is.

Apollo shone radiantly as ever, full of Olympian majesty and extending it around Orestes.

But the Furies walked through his barriers as if they did not exist. In a towering rage, he summoned his chariot, drawn by the fire-horses that drew it at his behest. He would have called on Father Zeus to smite the Furies with his thunderbolts. But Hermes appeared and whispered in his ear, then disappeared.

Humiliated, Apollo cast a spell to put the Furies to sleep. He could not fight them, but like Hermes, he could delay them. Then he whispered with Kalkhas and vanished. The seer approached Orestes and his party and told them,

"Lord Apollo has cast a spell to put the Furies to sleep. It will hold them for three days. Meanwhile, go to Athens and supplicate the goddess Athena for her protection. She is not there now, but Lord Hermes has gone to fetch her from her errands. It is to Athena in Athens that you must go."

Without another word, Orestes led his party out and got on the way to Attica and Athens. "So much for the promises of a god," he muttered. "And what if Athena fails?"

"His dreams were strong, and the headaches seemed real enough," Pylades said.

"You all do not have to come with me on this quest," Orestes said, shaking his head. "If Athena can save me, well and good. If even she cannot, the Furies will kill me whether anyone else is there or not."

"But Orestes," countered Pylades smiling. "We want to keep you company. Besides, I've never seen Athens. I believe that is true for everyone else."

"I've never been to Athens," declared Agathon, "I hear it is becoming a great city after Athena gave the people the gift of the olive tree. For that they chose her as their patron god over Poseidon..."

"I know what you men feel about the stories of the gods," hissed Elektra. "But don't even think it, let alone say it out loud."

"All right," agreed Agathon. "How about telling me the story of Hercules' pollution?"

Pylades guided his horse to Agathon's side and said, "As you know, Hercules was a favorite son of Zeus, although he was not born of Hera but of a mortal."

"But perhaps because he was not Hera's son," interjected Elektra, who had shared the tutor's lessons with the princes. "Hercules was a particular target of Hera's anger toward Zeus. Hera caused him to go mad and kill his wife and children."

"To cleanse himself of that ritual pollution, he had to perform those Twelve Labors, famous in our legends," concluded Pylades.

"Was that how he avoided those creatures?" asked Agathon.

"You mean the Erinyes, the Furies that are after Orestes?" Elektra added. "I think they might have taken into consideration Hera's role in making him mad."

"That would be logical," Pylades said. "Are the gods logical? Will Athena rely on logic?"

# 16: ATHENS AND CAPE SUNION

No one had expected much from the Athenians during the war against Troy. Many old tales spoke of the competition between Poseidon and Athena for the honor of being the presiding deity of the city. After the contest, Poseidon remained God of the seas and oceans, and the people accepted Athena as the Patron Goddess of the city. It was said that she presented the olive tree to the city.

One morning, the young royals and their companions from Delphi arrived in Athens and climbed up to Athena's shrine at the top of a hill. Orestes sat at the foot of the statue dedicated to the goddess of wisdom. That was as comfortable as one could be waiting on the floor of hewn rock in a shrine while clinging to the wooden statue of Athena. The priests seemed to know his needs and asked no questions.

At the bottom of a nearby hill, dedicated to the god Ares, was a new temple that housed the highest court in Athens. Judges there decided on crimes involving blood-guilt. Legends told of the trial of Ares himself for the murder of Poseidon's son.

"Well, you can go sightseeing now, Pylades, and anyone else who wants to go with you," said Orestes. "It will not be dangerous until the Furies get here. Not even Apollo can thwart them. I just hope that Athena can."

"We will be back before nightfall," said Pylades.

Elektra insisted on staying with her brother. "I want to watch the gods argue or whatever it is that they do." She brought water in pitchers from a nearby spring and spoke with the priests about bread before settling down for the afternoon.

\#

Agathon and the commander from Phocis returned first with a story of meeting some fishermen who lingered by the marketplace after they had sold all their fish. They were gossiping and told stories about Aegeas, the father of Theseus who organized a dozen villages into the city of Athens.

Pylades had gone to the same market with them but had joined a group of old soldiers who claimed to have been at Troy. They oohed and aahed when he spoke of Agamemnon's sword but scoffed at his story of Iphigenia's death. Instead they told the story of Erechtheos, an ancient king of Athens. He had fought many battles against competitors for the territory of the city. His daughters, they claimed, volunteered to die as sacrifices to the gods to secure the city for their father.

"That's sacrilegious!" exclaimed Elektra. "Our gods do not demand such sacrifices."

"Some old warriors thought so as well," said Pylades with a shrug.

#

The space inside Athena's temple pulsed with dense shadows that shimmered. The torches flickered but did not go out. A smell of old dirt like that they encountered in Delphi suffused the small hall. The Fates appeared out of the thin air.

Then, Orestes' party felt as if the sunshine and breezes of the hillside were in the building with them. Athena appeared to face the Fates. They seemed to resume the argument that Apollo had abandoned.

[*The Furies*]

To let matricide go unpunished
Would unseat the foundation
Of Right and set Evil loose on
The world unbridled and uncurbed

By Fear or Shame, Conscience or Honor.

[*Athena*]

I believe that Apollo has cleansed Orestes of what
You call pollution, but his guilt for shedding of blood
Must be weighed by men in a new way, by laws.
No more shall a killing begat another as of
Old—a grim unending spiral, as taking an eye
For an eye would rob the whole world of sight.
Therefore, in Athens, by my command, twelve men
Shall judge; hearing all witnesses and fearing no one.
They shall sit in a temple built here on Ares' hill,
To deliberate and vote each man as Reason shall lead.
Should their votes be split equally, the casting vote
Shall be mine; that is all the prerogative I claim,
By Zeus. To these judges now belong the burden
Of determining guilt when any sheds blood anywhere.
This is now the process, I pray you to consent,
To let men decide instead of passion or gods.

[*The Furies*]

This is too new for us. We grasp
Not the reason nor the desired
Outcome. Do you think to make
Men good by enacting more laws?
What is gained for gods or men
By waiting upon the verdict of twelve?
Men will lose their sense of conscience,
Of shame before other men, of
Fear for giving offense to gods
Or tradition. Will they respect

Your new laws? For their nature will
Not change. What new reverence will
The gods or men gain?

[*Athena*]

Father Zeus has decreed that I should so devise
The laws and practice that must prevail to guide
Men in their lives together in cities. Borders for farms
And boundaries for behavior. Clear principles
By which to devise and frame them; due processes
For resolving dispute and adjudicating
Wrong-doing with or without intent—that man
And all society may flourish and prosper.
Thus here twelve men will decide the guilt of my
Supplicant, Orestes, whether or not with cause.

The Athenian court, meeting on Ares' hill, split its votes at six
each for and against acquittal. Athena cast her vote to break
the tie—

[*Athena*]

Not having had a mother myself, but born out of
Father Zeus' head full grown and completely armed,
I hereby cast my vote for the man you accuse.
Let us set him free forthwith of all guilt and stain.

[*The Furies*]

This troubles us, we smell trickery.
Our displeasure could turn venomous
And spill on this fair land of yours.

Much misery shall come of this;
Is this what the younger gods have
Decided on—total war between
The generations of the gods?

[*Athena*]

It was a fair vote as you saw, one you nearly won.
There was no treachery involved, my vote was cast
Openly; nor did I try to sway any of the
Judges. Be not hasty to wage war with younger
Gods, for we are stronger than you, Zeus' thunderbolts
Are within my reach, I know where He hides them.

[*The Furies*]

Do you now threaten us with force?
Our quarrel would create such waste,
Pestilence and blight around,
That you could never call it peace.

[*Athena*]

I did not mean to threaten you but to persuade;
If you would let go of your anger and forswear the
Plague. Come rest here among these mountain rocks and huts,
I will share the reverence offered by these folks.

[*The Furies*]

First threats, now bribes, your disrespect
Dishonors both you and us. Such
Insolence, such contempt, is that

What you offer those defeated?

[*Athena*]

Not disrespect nor contempt, but what I have I would
Share: the reverence of the good people here.
Do not look down on these rocks and huts for someday
A bright future I foresee, you who are old and wise
Can see it too. These poor mountain slopes and valleys
Will ring with glorious words and deeds beyond compare.

[*The Furies*]

O'erwhelmed, dishonored and crushed, yet we
Can pour forth venom, blight
And bane. Not that such is comfort
To our wounded pride and joy.

[*Athena*]

Then share in our delight, the pride and reverence of all
Who dwell in these woods and farms—their births and deaths,
Their every breath shall be a prayer to your honored
Presence. Forsake your venom and bile; let your
Blessing instead grace these rocks and huts with me.
Do not bring blight when you can bring hope and good cheer.

[*The Furies*]

You speak sweet words, but what will you,
What can you do and for how long?
Do all the younger gods agree:
Ares, Apollo, and Father Zeus?

[*Athena*]

If you all agree, I may speak for them all.
Those who worship you shall receive my blessing.
My sanctuary shall be your sanctuary, my shrine
Your shrine. It shall be so forever—Forever.

[*The Furies*]

Then we accept your offer thus
Made with dignity and courtesy.
We must warn you nevertheless
That though we accept our path
To fade away—the day will come
When gods and men will rue this day
That reason and the rule of law
O'er-shadowed extravagant honor
And the terrors, the pangs of conscience.
Walls and rules to replace fame
Or shame or fear, passion or pain!
*Ou-ai! Ou-ai!* The day will come,
You will wish the Erinyes were still
With you and your farms and cities.

The verdict relieved the young royals, their escort was
jubilant. The much conflicted Agathon now expressed the
wish to visit the sea. "I've heard Cape Sunion was where an
ancient king of Athenian songs and legends killed himself and
I should like to see such a place." The idea appealed even to
Orestes, now relieved his ordeal was over. The full realization
of his actions—the killing of Aigisthos and of his mother—

increasingly troubled him, however, and his heart yearned for the distraction.

Agathon went to get supplies for their trip. It was a full day's ride and, at the cape, they camped on a cliff to watch as the fishing boats sailed back to shore and the sun set, dipping it seemed into the sea. They made camp by the glittering light of the stars.

#

"Theseus had promised his father to hoist white sails if he returned from Crete victorious over the Minotaur. He was successful with the help of Ariadne, the Cretan princess, but in the excitement he forgot the sails and left the black ones in place. His father threw himself off the Akropolis," explained Pylades.

"It was Theseus who unified the different parts of Attica," added Elektra, "as our great-grandfather Pelops did for the Argolid and surrounding areas. I wonder if they ever met."

The constellations wheeled slowly but inexorably through the night as distant waves crashed and lapped on the shore beneath the cliff. Orestes felt a strange calm as he watched the sky roll on. How, he wondered, had he moved beyond the agonizing doubt of the past year before his wretched deeds in Mycenae and the bitter guilt of the previous weeks after those heinous acts?

# EPILOGUE

A subdued band of riders made their way from Athens to Phocis. Agathon had excused himself when the road forked and bade them farewell, for he would ride back to Mycenae. "Look for me in Phocis in twenty days."

Strophios and Anaxibia welcomed the young royals. At a banquet two nights later, Strophios announced that he would like to step down and have Pylades become king in his place. Orestes winced and withdrew further into himself. He was not surprised, but that did not soften the wrenching anguish he felt.

Then Pylades stood up and walked over to Elektra, who blushed deeply. Carefully avoiding Orestes' eyes, he announced to all present that he would marry Elektra on the same day as his coronation. The priests would determine what day would be most propitious. Orestes somehow summoned up the self-control to walk over to his sister and kiss her. Then he announced that as future king of Mycenae, he would be proud to have such a brave and faithful ally as his new brother-in-law. When they left after dinner, Pylades looked over at Elektra, and in that exchange of looks, the prince told his bride-to-be he was about to spend his last hour with his lover. With a strained nod, Elektra gave him her approval. He slid his hand lovingly into Orestes' and guided him to their former chambers.

Orestes' lips trembled, and his tears began to flow even as they arrived. Pylades embraced him and kissed him as when they had first met. When the Mycenaean prince had given vent to all his desolation and misery, he gathered himself and stated, "Goodbye, my brother, my love. I will do my best to come to your coronation, but I hope you will forgive me if I should find myself unable to stay for your wedding. Know also that you and Elektra hold all the love that I am, or ever have been, capable of." His lips trembled but his voice was firm, and he left the room that instant with resolution.

The next day, as he set off for Delphi, his uncle Strophios was there to send him off. The king nodded to the commander who had accompanied the young royals on their recent frenzied journeys, and the soldier fell in two or three horse lengths behind Orestes. The prince realized that, much as he wished to be alone, there would be occasions when he would be glad of the company.

Nearing Delphi, the two men stopped to gaze at the grove of birch trees. The young prince absorbed the sight of the woods with their splendid silvery trunks. They sang to him as mermaids are said to sing to sailors, luring them to strange waters. To Orestes, it seemed he had found the balm to soothe his raw emotions. The prospect of separation from Pylades, his companion and lover for fifteen summers, wrenched his soul from even the memory of murdering his mother. The song of the birches was the unguent to sweeten the gall of such a rupture.

Kalkhas welcomed Orestes with evident satisfaction and made him comfortable in Apollo's shrine. The prince spent time in solitude in the shrine and on leisurely rides through the nearby woods. The seer did not appear disconcerted even when he visited the community of Dionysius followers.

Agathon arrived back in Mycenae in time for the funeral ceremonies for the late king and queen. He spent a whole day in tears and in prayer at Aigisthos' memorial, pouring libation after libation as if he was pouring out his heart. The young soldier was unable to make sense of ritual pollution, the gods, Hercules' labors, or the emotions conjured up by his loyalty sworn to the coming king. He poured out his heart in unaffected grief for the only king he had yet ever known.

The next day, he and his family accompanied his mother to the house of her sister-in-law, the widow of the night watchman. The old man had died in his sleep a few days after the news about Aigisthos and Clytemnestra scorched Mycenae. "He left you his spear and his prayer that you would serve faithfully in the guards. He mourned for the King briefly and then died peacefully with his grandchildren all by his side."

Two days later, Agathon attached the banner of a herald to his spear and cantered to Phocis. Twelve soldiers and counselor Aristides rode with him, for they would return with the new king of Mycenae.

# CAST OF CHARACTERS

The following is a list and brief description of the characters involved in the Greek legend during its classical period, in the Oresteia, and in Agamemnon Must Die. They are not listed alphabetically but are grouped by "generations." Names of those significant in this retelling are in capitals.

**The royals:**
First generation
Atreus, king of Mycenae, was married to Aerope and was the father of AGAMEMNON, Menelaos, and Anaxibia. His brother was Thyestes.

Thyestes, who lost the kingship of Mycenae to Atreus, was the father of two young sons butchered by Atreus, a daughter, Pelopia, and AIGISTHOS, his son by Pelopia.

Tyndareos, king of Sparta, was the father of CLYTEMNESTRA and Helen (of Troy), who married Atreus' sons. He abdicated in favor of his son-in-law, Menelaos.

Second generation
AGAMEMNON, king of Mycenae after his father, was the husband of CLYTEMNESTRA, and father of Iphigenia, ORESTES, and ELEKTRA.

Menelaos, king of Sparta, was AGAMEMNON's brother and married to Helen.

Anaxibia, Atreus' daughter, was married to Strophios, king of Phocis. She was PYLADES' mother.

AIGISTHOS, son of Thyestes, was thus Agamemnon's cousin. He was abandoned at birth but found and brought to the palace, where Atreus and Aerope raised him as their youngest son.

CLYTEMNESTRA, queen of Mycenae, was the mother of Iphigenia, ORESTES, and ELEKTRA.

Third generation
Cassandra, one of the daughters of Priam, king of Troy, and sister to Hector and Paris, was a captive brought back by Agamemnon as his war trophy.

ORESTES, son of AGAMEMNON, was sent with his sister ELEKTRA to live with his aunt Anaxibia when his mother CLYTEMNESTRA took AIGISTHOS as her lover. Seven years after his father AGAMEMNON was killed, he returned to Mycenae to avenge the regicide.

ELEKTRA, ORESTES' sister, and PYLADES, his lover, accompanied him on his journey of vengeance.

**The non-royals**:
Kalkhas, the seer and faithful servant of the god Apollo, accompanied the Greeks to Troy and returned to assist ORESTES.

ARISTIDES, one of the Elders of Mycenae (not named in Aeschylus' play).

AGATHON, the herald (also not named in Aeschylus' play) became a valued member of the Mycenaean palace guards, and was ordered by AIGISTHOS to protect ORESTES.

The NIGHT WATCHMAN is an important character in this book, even though he is not named.

**The Immortals**:
APOLLO, son of Zeus, Olympian god of prophecy.
HERMES, son of Zeus, Olympian messenger god.
ATHENA, daughter of Zeus, Olympian goddess of wisdom.
THE FURIES / ERINYES, older than Zeus, they belong to a previous generation of immortals and protect sacred customs.

# FURTHER READING

The Oresteia has been translated into English many times, even recently (fifteen since Robert Fagles' in 1975), and I have read several of these translations. These are listed here in the event others wish to see what might have gone into *Agamemnon Must Die*.

Johnston, Ian, 2002, online.
Lattimore, R. 1942. (This is usually found in The Complete Greek Tragedies, edited by David Grene and Richmond Lattimore and published 1959).
Morshead, E. D. A., 1909
Smyth, H. W. Now available on-line, Smyth's translation most famously appears with the Greek text in Harvard's Loeb Classics.
Theodoridis, G. 2005, online.

Of the more recent translations that I did not read, I have noticed strong feelings expressed among readers about those by
Robert Fagles, 1975 and
Ted Hughes, 1999 (published posthumously).

I have also availed myself of the learning and wisdom of
Bowra, C. M. *The Greek Experience*, 1957.
Conacher, D. J. *Aeschylus' Oresteia, a literary commentary*. 1987.
Connelly, Joan Breton. *The Parthenon Enigma*. 2014.
Graves, Robert, *The White Goddess*, 1948.
Jaeger, W., trans. G. Highet, *Paideia: The Ideals of Greek Culture*, 1939-44.
Kuhns, R. *The House, the City and the Judge*. 1962.
Lattimore, R. "Introduction," to David Grene and R. Lattimore, cds., *The Complete Greek Tragedies*, 1942.
Vellacott, Philip, *The Logic of Tragedy*, 1984.

In pursuit of a graduate degree in history, I also read many other works on Greek history. Alas, I no longer remember any particular insight put forward by any specific author.

# ABOUT THE AUTHOR

Hock G. Tjoa was born in Singapore to Chinese parents. He studied history at Brandeis and Harvard and taught European history and Asian political thought at the University of Malaya in Kuala Lumpur. He has published George Henry Lewes, a Victorian Mind, "The social and political ideas of Tan Cheng Lock" (in Melaka: The Transformation of a Malay Capital) and various articles in the Newsletter of the China History Forum. He is married and lives with his family in the Sierra Nevada foothills of California.

In 2010, he published The Battle of Chibi, selections translated from "The Romance of the Three Kingdoms" (one of four traditional Chinese classic novels). In 2011, he adapted Lao She's "Tea House," Mandarin original dated 1953, publishing it as Heaven is High and the Emperor Far Away, a Play. Both are part of his goal to contribute to a wider and greater understanding of China and Asia. Earlier in 2013, he published The Chinese Spymaster, the first he hopes in a trilogy of contemporary spy novels. Later that year, he published The Ingenious Judge Dee, a Play.

The Author's blog is hockgtjoa.blogspot.com
His website is www.sleepingdragonbooks.com
He tweets very occasionally and can be reached via Twitter @hgtjoa

His email address is tjoa.books@gmail.com

# OTHER BOOKS BY THE AUTHOR

(in alphabetical order)

*The Battle of Chibi,* selections translated from the "Romance of the Three Kingdoms" (by Luo Guanzhong, ca. 1400), 2010, second edition (Sleeping Dragon Press) 2016.
*The Chinese Spymaster*, 2013.
*Heaven is High and the Emperor Far Away, A Play*, adapted from "Teahouse," by Lao She (Shu Qingchun, 1899-1966) in 2011.
*The Ingenious Judge Dee, a Play*, 2013, adapted from The Celebrated Cases of Judge Dee, an 18th century Chinese "detective novel," translated in 1949 by Robert van Gulik.
*The Ninja and the Diplomat*, volume 2 of The Chinese Spymaster,

# EXTRACTS from other writing

## FROM THE BATTLE OF CHIBI

Long ago, along a stretch of a river deep and wide but far away from the consciousness or imagination of anyone outside All under Heaven (China), a battle was fought that determined the unity of the empire for the next four hundred years. It was there along the Yangzi that Liu Bei, the Loyalist, and Zhou Yu, commander in chief of Wu, the kingdom established by the most successful of the Chinese warlords, defeated Cao Cao, the Usurper. In defeating Cao's huge army and armada, Bei and Yu established Shu and Wu as powers together with Cao's Wei that would divide China into the Three Kingdoms.

The south bank of that stretch of river was called Chibi, Red Cliffs, and that name was given to the battle. Cao was forced to flee northwards back to his base; he regrouped his forces and, by virtue of holding the last Han Emperor hostage and of having the largest body of men in arms, remained the "First Man" of China, but he was never again able to threaten South China.

The Romance of the Three Kingdoms asserts in its very first chapter the Chinese view of history—not as a linear progression from primitive to developed (first-world status), but as an alternation between the unity of the Chinese Empire and political chaos, "disunity." It was a major achievement of Zhuge Liang to persuade his contemporaries that China could exist as a triangular balance of power—Loyalists, Usurpers and Wu/Jiangdong. Thus, after four hundred years of imperial unity under the Han dynasty, China came to be ruled by the Three Kingdoms. These kingdoms lasted only eighty years that with the three centuries that followed (before the establishment of a unified China by the Sui and Tang dynasties) became known as the Age of Fragmentation.

The Romance and hence this work are not merely about the military actions or political considerations of that era, but also about values. Perhaps the most crucial question was the implication for loyal subjects when Fate appears to have determined that a dynasty should end. (By the Ming dynasty, this was codified and thus resolved, but the Romance reflects the uncertain tension before such a resolution.) For many intellectuals, this conflict prompted a desire for the "contemplative life," reflecting perhaps an escapist yearning, perhaps the quietist aspect of Daoist thought. This preference is mixed with a sense of fatalism. Zhuge Liang is unafraid when he is in Wu/Jiangdong because the end of his life has been decreed by Fate--but he also planned meticulously for his final escape from Wu on board a boat that he orders a month in advance.

To tell of his many stratagems is to learn that, for Liang, not everything has been written in the Book of Fate or if it had, there was still the possibility that with enough effort and the right angle of vision, one might change the course of Fate. Liang's vision was to see China neither as an empire nor in chaos, as enunciated in the opening paragraph of the Romance; did he believe that it could be ruled by three kingdoms and for a while he was successful. Perhaps he dared to think that this would enable him and "All under Heaven" to escape "Fate." To achieve this, however, he "coughed up his life's blood."

Part of the price to pay was a continued battle of wits between Liang and Zhou Yu of Jiangdong. This battle was itself a continuation of the vendetta between the two regions since Sun Jian, the patriarch of Jiangdong, was confronted by Liu Biao, Bei's kinsman and protector while he ruled Jingzhou; all retold in this volume. After Biao's death, the dispute became one over territory—Jingzhou, which the Wu kingdom of Jiangdong regarded as an extension of its realm.

The vendetta did not end with the death of Zhou Yu although this retelling of the Romance does, closing with Yu's funeral at which Liang mourns with a moving eulogy.

From the Back Cover of the Battle of Chibi

"Fascinating insight into a whole new world of thought."
Hasan S. Padamsee, Professor of Physics, Cornell, NY.

"Lively and entertaining translation of a Chinese classic that deserves a wide audience."
Beryl S. Slocum, Salve Regina University, RI.

"Excellent translation, faithful to the spirit of the Romance as I recall from reading it many times (in Korean)."
Seung-il Shin, formerly Professor of Genetics, Albert Einstein College of Medicine, NY.

"Opens new vistas of fascinating history and thought."
Susan Wilson, Sierra College Library, CA.


EXTRACT FROM The Chinese Spymaster, volume 1: Operation Kashgar

PROLOGUE
(A suburb of Beijing)

It has been said that thought makes one wise. In hand to hand combat, however, thinking kills.

Spymaster Wang clasped his right fist in his left hand and made a slight bow as Sergeant Major Li reciprocated. Both men were alike in being slim and nearly six feet tall. Wang, however, was in his early fifties, and the sparring sessions were his self-imposed tests of physical fitness. Li was not quite 30, a trainer of army special forces in the finer art of close combat. Immediately the two men began a series of slow arm and body motions. They might have been those of ordinary men and women at their morning taijiquan exercises that could be observed in a park in any Chinese city. As they moved around each other in the bare, medium-sized room used for Wang's weekly test in hand to hand combat, the pace of their movements increased until they were so fast that fists, arms and legs were all a blur.

Li made several flying and spinning kicks. At times, he used a wall or two for leverage or positioning. His blows were aimed at particular pressure points. Had these landed precisely, they would have inflicted serious bodily damage as well as pain. Some of them could have maimed or even killed the Spymaster. The style of fighting that focused on attacking an opponent's pressure points left them with unblemished faces, but their bodies were usually covered with painful bruises after each session. Li's footwork was sure, and no observer could have doubted or mistaken the force behind his feet, fists, and knuckles.

Wang forced his mind to empty itself of all thought.

Act without desiring the results of your action!

Japanese Zen Masters taught this mantra. Chinese Chan Masters had taught the Zen Masters, and they had learned this kernel of insight that pre-dated Lord Buddha himself. But there were so many thoughts that demanded Wang's attention; and a lifetime of deep and disciplined thinking distinguished him from most of his predecessors and peers. Nevertheless, for now, this was the imperative of combat. The combatants relied on instinct, intuition, "muscle memory," gongfu, qi.

A swift thrust from Li connected. He barely missed one of those pressure points as Wang made just a small sideways jerk at the last split-second. The Spymaster winced even as he continued the whirring ballet of combat. His movements could not compare in speed and athleticism with those of the Sergeant's. He moved more economically, mostly to deflect the thrusts and kicks that the Sergeant sent in a ceaseless, apparently effortless, barrage. Once or twice, Wang whipped out a jab or slashing blow. He usually connected, though never at the intended target points. Li grunted at those instances.

Why am I doing this?

The thought burst through Wang's grimly controlled consciousness of a void in space-time. But this thought was only a dangerous distraction. Nothing could exist for either man except the ebb and flow and eddies of their movements. Movements fast enough to be indistinct, balletic, potentially lethal.

These weekly bouts were observed by no one. Few even knew they took place. General Chen, of a nearby army corps, was one who did. Wang had asked him two years earlier for a new sparring partner, and Chen had searched among those who trained his own men in hand to hand combat. He found and recommended the Sergeant Major, who then made his weekly visits to the Spymaster's offices. Chen was among the handful of men that the Spymaster really trusted. They had been schoolmates for a decade, and the bonds forged between ages five and fifteen had survived subsequent decades of separate political education and military training. On rare occasions, they called on each other for favors, usually when survival was at stake and such favors were critical, maybe even perilous. Finding and recommending Sergeant Li had not seemed to be such a favor.

Then, a few weeks earlier, Chen discovered that Li had a well-concealed obligation to Comrade Commissar Jiang, someone known to nurse a vicious grudge against Wang. The friends believed this was because Wang had declined to appoint a Jiang protégé as his deputy. When he learned about the obligation, Chen immediately relayed the information to his friend and was startled that Wang chose to continue the weekly exercises. Chen and Wang had so far been unable to find a convenient occasion to discuss this distressing matter.

Li also concentrated on keeping his mind from distracting his body. He was fully confident in his skill as the best trainer in hand to hand combat in General Chen's army corps. Even though he had never defeated the Spymaster in the two years of their weekly training sessions, he knew he had the edge in strength and speed. He also knew that, despite lingering bruises, he usually recovered by the next day from each sparring session, while the Spymaster occasionally carried a sore spot or two from a prior week's encounter. What distracted him most this day, however, was that he had received word from Comrade Commissar Jiang two weeks before that it was time to "accidentally" kill or cripple the Spymaster. In the previous two exercises with the Spymaster, he had not yet found a way physically—or morally—to do so.

Li decided to attack Wang's legs with a series of kicks. The knees were vulnerable, and he hoped that Wang would not be agile enough to avoid all his blows. Wang responded with kicks of his own and occasionally executed a leg sweep. Li expected the effort to move from an upright position to the floor and back again would tire Wang out quickly. Yet, Wang kept up with Li, kick for kick. He blocked and jabbed at Li's head and chest to distract the Sergeant. But this session would not last as long as their usual sparring sessions.

Li remained in control of the tempo of the fight. He switched back from the attack on Wang's legs and drove the Spymaster into a corner of the room with a series of kicks and knuckle jabs. Wang deflected this barrage with a graceful combination of arm sweeps and pivots away from the attack. Suddenly, Spymaster Wang lashed out with a forceful knuckle jab of his own. It was the only one of his blows that completely missed the Sergeant. Li ducked and twisted away. He launched himself up one wall then crossed over to another and landed perfectly positioned to send a flying kick directly at the Spymaster's sternum. This kick would kill.

This time, the Spymaster could not block or twist away; his misjudged jab left him too far off-balance to do either. He just had time enough to brace himself and block the Sergeant's attacking foot. He caught it half an inch from his chest. Without pausing or thinking, the Sergeant swung his other foot away to build sufficient momentum to wrench his foot out of the Spymaster's two-handed grasp. He landed far enough away that it signaled the end of the combat exercise.

Both men remained in control of their breathing and bowed slightly to each other.

"Thank you, Sergeant Major. It was an excellent exercise."

"Thank you, Spymaster. I am honored."

"You let me off three times during our match."

"Actually, sir, it was five times. But you let me off twice."

"In battle, one does what one must do 'in the moment.' Who knows what might have happened if either of us had pressed our advantages as they appeared?"

"Combat is full of uncertainty."

The Spymaster smiled grimly. "Perhaps I am getting too old for this."

The Sergeant Major also smiled, a small smile, and replied, "I can think of none of your companions who could have lasted as long in this room."

"Next week, we shall meet in another place. I shall let you know where, but you should come as if to this room."

The Sergeant Major understood the significance of this request; he was to be unarmed. He was not worried, for he knew that his life had always been in Wang's hands. The Spymaster commanded resources against which a dozen armed men would not prevail in a frontal attack, perhaps not even a dozen armored divisions. Li's only opportunity to fulfill his promise to Comrade Commissar Jiang was during one of the weekly sparring sessions. But he closed his mind to those thoughts—his fate would be decided between the Spymaster and the Comrade Commissar.

The Spymaster, on the other hand, now allowed himself the luxury of thought as he left the combat room and made his way briskly to his office. He would shower and change on the way, stopping briefly at the infirmary for the usual balms and poultices, as well as the customary scolding from his old school teacher, now the chief medical officer at the agency, who thought Wang should stop putting himself in harm's way.

Prioritize!

Do I need a bodyguard?

What about Sergeant Major Li?

What does Comrade Commissar Jiang really want?

What do I say at the Committee on Public Security meeting in two days—especially in light of the new activity in "Operation Kashgar"?

Extract from volume 2 in the series, The Ninja and the Diplomat

CHAPTER 1
Sunday in Macau

"Room service."

Kim, the North Korean arms dealer, looked at his bodyguard across the ample rosewood and silk chairs in the living room of his suite and motioned with his head for him to get the door.

"We did not order anything."

"Compliments of Viktor."

The arms dealer hesitated then nodded. His bodyguard opened the door cautiously and waved a metal detecting wand over the man as he wheeled in a polished wooden cart laden with fruit. A basket of fresh local lychees, grown in carefully chosen orchards within two hundred miles of Macau, sat beside cut-up mangoes from the Philippines on ice; a plate of custard tarts in fluffy pastry shells; truffles exquisitely crafted by the hotel's own chocolatier; the plum and marzipan crumble that was the establishment's signature dessert, and the customary bottle of champagne in an ice bucket, Veuve Clicquot Yellow Brut. Viktor knew that to really impress Kim he should have ordered the Cave Privee but there was a limit to his expense account.

"You really should try the egg tarts. They are better than those in Hong Kong," purred a heavily accented voice from outside the door. Viktor entered and made himself at home. He gestured for the champagne and took a glass asserting, "No tampering in any of this, I assure you."

He breathed in deeply, looked around the room discriminately and nodded with approval. The light floral scent in the room came from real flowers, the aroma of chocolate and butter arose from the truffles, and the furnishings announced not the showy affluence of shirts newly taken out of their wrappings or cars just driven off the show room floor but the well-maintained and self-assured comfort of a high-end but reserved resort.

The man from room service was a local, so Kim and his bodyguards could assume he was not from Viktor's "inner circle." However, Viktor notoriously used gangs of local organized crime. He snatched a knife from the cart and attacked the bodyguard. Even though there was a crazed look in his eyes, suggesting he was under the influence of some drug, he wielded the knife with skill. It was, however, as if a lucky beginner was fighting a hardened professional. The guard had to dodge three or four times before blocking a knife thrust with the metal detector and striking the attacker's throat. The attacker arched backwards while slashing at the outstretched arm. The guard spun to avoid the knife and caught the attacker by the wrist. He swung the man effortlessly into a wall against which he crashed and lay crumpled.

As the attacker slumped to the floor, another man moved silently into the doorway. "Was that too easy?" he asked as he raised his silenced Glock 19, the compact version of the ubiquitous hand-gun. He shot at the bodyguard, who sprang at the same instant to relative safety behind the furniture in the living room.

Kim wasted no time in firing his 9 mm Beretta which he favored over the Glock because of its heft. He did not miss, not even when a second gunman rushed into the room.

"Your marksmanship has improved greatly," remarked Viktor as he casually drew his own weapon, "but there are three more of us and we have something..."

There was a short pause as guns clattered and curses were muttered. A door had opened near the staircase down the hall.

A shrill whistle blew.

"Stop! Police. Drop your weapons."

The arrival of the police surprised everyone inside and outside the suite of rooms at the quietly stylish hotel that had served as Kim's base of operations. Even so, he maintained his usual calm facade as Viktor and his crew cursed. The police brought with them the odor of officious authority that blended well with the whiff of sulfur and cordite.

Within a few minutes, all the attackers and those attacked were taken, separately, into custody.